Private Fame

ILLINOIS SHORT FICTION

A list of books in the series appears at the end of this volume.

Richard Burgin

Private Fame

UNIVERSITY OF ILLINOIS PRESS

Urbana and Chicago

Publication of this work was supported in part by grants from the Illinois Arts Council, a state agency, and the National Endowment for the Arts.

The author wishes to thank Richard and Julia Breslin, Thomas L. Canavan, Andrew Levy, Ann Lowry, Rafal Olbinski, Burton Porter, Terry Sears, Constance Decker Thompson, Andre Zarre, and a special thanks to Linda K. Harris.

Manufactured in the United States of America
C 5 4 3 2 1

This book is printed on acid-free paper.

"The Spirit of New York," an earlier version appeared in *Witness* 4:1 (1990)
"Psycho in Buckingham Palace," *Mississippi Review* 16:1 (1988); listed among the year's best stories in *Pushcart Prize XIV: Best of the Small Presses*
"Rats," an earlier version appeared in *OnTheBus* 5 (1991)
"Silver Screen," an earlier version appeared in *Mississippi Review* 36 (Spring 1984)
"Heidi Indoors," original version appeared in *Kansas Quarterly* 18:1-2 (Winter-Spring 1986); a revised version appeared in *Boulevard* 3:2-3 (Fall 1988); listed among the year's best stories in *Pushcart Prize XII: Best of the Small Presses*
"Vivian and Sid," *Denver Quarterly* (forthcoming)
"Some Notes toward Ending Time," an earlier version appeared in *Fiction* 6:3 (1981)
"Peacock Farm," *Kansas Quarterly* 23:1-2 (Winter-Spring 1991)
"Song of the Earth," an earlier version appeared (under the title "Private Fame") in *Prospect Review* 1:1 (September 1990)
"The Horror Age," *Another Chicago Magazine* 23 (Spring 1991)
"From the Diary of Gene Mays," *TriQuarterly* 81 (June 1991)

Library of Congress Cataloging-in-Publication Data

Burgin, Richard.
    Private fame / Richard Burgin.
        p.   cm. — (Illinois short fiction)
    ISBN 0-252-01843-5 (alk. paper)
    I. Title. II. Series.
PS3552.U717P7 1991
813'.54—dc20   91-6331
                                                                          CIP

*To my mother
and to Linda*

Contents

Looking back, it's hard to remember how I felt in the aftermath of scaring Karen. For one thing, I don't remember spending even a minute trying to understand why I scared her or why I derived so much pleasure from it. Maybe I simply understood it all as a natural expression of my being, and the fact that I lost Karen as a result, as well as any happiness at the beach for the rest of the summer, made me feel I'd paid the price.

And yet, two summers later, at Cape Cod (my parents were restless vacationers), I struck again. This time it was with a little brunette I'd befriended for a few days named Margie, who was probably about ten. Unfortunately, Margie must have told her daddy, for when I bicycled past her cottage looking for her the next day he immediately came after me in his car. His lecture to me (on the soft shoulder, while some very curious drivers whizzed by) was pretty frightening itself, culminating in a promise to kill me if I ever scared his little Margie again. I nodded piously and apologized. As I pedaled away, I tried to dismiss him as a fanatic, but I did keep away from his daughter and the beach in general for the rest of the summer.

In fact, Cape Cod Daddy did such a good job of scaring me that for the next five years I put all my energy into schoolwork, instead of scaring people, and wound up at a quite prestigious college near Boston.

Then in my sophomore year, love tracked me down, just jumped out at me and set me spinning. Her name was Michelle, like the old Beatles song. She was nervous, delicate, sensuous, eager to please. Michelle was many things; that was my first surprise. My next was that our sex life was so paradoxically disappointing. I'd imagined that sex with someone you love would inevitably lead to prolonged states of rapturous closeness. I had the romantic notion that the physical climax was merely the prelude to a much longer-lasting ecstasy. Instead, more often than not, the spiritual bliss I sought died with the physical or shortly thereafter, as if our timid souls were programmed to flee each other rather than to experience too much pleasure. Our lovemaking was like a play we'd memorized, where each of us performed our roles night after night with only the slightest variation. At the time I blamed Michelle, though I now believe it's an intrinsic limitation of the sex act itself, or else of so-called human nature.

Because of this unexpected yet inescapable disappointment, I suggested a new game to Michelle. The two of us could play it in my parents' house, for they were often traveling and I'd long ago smuggled away a key. The game was a variation on hide and seek, and Michelle, of course, said she'd certainly try it.

At first I believed I would follow the rules of the game I'd, after all, devised myself. According to the rules, the hider (usually me) would jump out and embrace the seeker once the latter had discovered his whereabouts, and then begin to make love in whatever spot he was occupying. The first time we played, my parents were safely away at some convention for business lawyers. I hid in one of their bathrooms, a space so impersonal I couldn't tell which of them it belonged to. (I certainly knew it wasn't used by both of them since they lived in separate rooms and, except for their compulsive traveling, did everything separately.) I shut myself in the closet beside some cleaning fluids and a series of neutral looking, though spotlessly clean, towels.

I could hear Michelle whistling as she searched for me, and then singing some silly songs designed to make me laugh and give away my whereabouts. But I was already succumbing to something more powerful than laughter. At first I felt frightened. Then the old thrill of hiding and anticipating, of planning my scream and my jump flashed through me. Though five years had passed, I simply couldn't struggle against it and was literally quivering with excitement.

After scaring Michelle I was so elated that I found I had to think of her expression when I first scared her in order to keep up my lovemaking.

Needless to say, the game, which was supposed to be a variation, soon became a regular feature of our love life. When my parents' house wasn't available we played a scaled-down version in my studio apartment, and when the hiding spots there became too predictable, we'd take a room in a hotel; or in the warm weather we'd rent a car and drive out to the country. The Berkshires—in fact, Beachwood itself—could be reached with a very enjoyable two-and-a-half-hour drive.

I found no reason to tell Michelle why I wanted to play there in the grove at night. I was feeling too much excitement then to delve into my past, having little patience for either guilt or analysis. I rationalized it all this way: we are both consenting adults. I love the game, and by choosing to keep playing it, she indicates that she must like it, too. Although by the time of our trip to Beachwood there was a lot of contradictory evidence on that point. At first Michelle thought of the game as kinky. She thought we were pioneers creating an avant-garde mix of sex and theater, but the repetition had frayed her nerves. She had complained once, snapped at me a couple of times, and had let tears well up in her eyes the last few times I'd suggested playing.

Around ten o'clock, after checking into a hotel in nearby Lenox, we drove down the dirt road that led to the grove and the infamous bathhouses. We parked just outside the grove in a grassy area by a creek and walked toward it on a winding path, each armed with a flashlight. There were many stars out, but the trees overhead were so high and dense we felt we were walking in total darkness.

Michelle had been ominously quiet for some time. When she nearly tripped over a stray branch, she started to cry a little, then quickly said, "I don't want to do this."

"Michelle, calm down. We're safe. Our car's thirty yards away."

She stopped crying but repeated her objection.

"It will only take a few minutes," I said. "We'll play a short game. I'll give you clues."

"I'm already scared. I don't need to play the game to be scared."

"But there's nothing to be scared of."

"*You're* scaring me," she said firmly, and I knew then that we were headed back to the car and to a long analytical discussion. I wasn't surprised that we drove back to Boston the next morning after fighting all night long, and that the trial separation she suggested turned into a permanent one.

After I lost Michelle, for a long time there was no one. I reacted to my personal tragedy as I had before, by redoubling my efforts at school, and then at the New York advertising agency where I'd begun writing copy for accounts including an airline, a specially shaped toothbrush, and (appropriately enough) a bathroom cleanser. At the agency we were trying to make the public desire our products, but we were also trying to make them fear the consequences of *not* buying them. I couldn't help recognizing this strange coupling of fear and desire everywhere in New York, even in the clothes people wore. People dressed to make an impression, but they were clearly dressing to scare each other too. From the dapper young executives at the power lunches to the hookers on the street, the message was, "Look at me. Take me in carefully (though not too carefully) with your eyes. Can you really afford *not* to buy what I'm selling? Can you really feel safe existing without me?" The effect of it all was to make me withdraw even more.

Before I lived there, I'd often thought of New York as one of the images of infinity. (Infinity was a concept that had dazzled me throughout my adolescence.) But now I found that, while conceptually beautiful, infinity is more terrifying than anything else. You cannot defend against endlessness; it breaks down every system. I was particularly ill suited to try. The landscapes of my life were the lake and grove of Beachwood, my suburban college campus, and my parents' scrupulously neat home, where I used to daydream about the size of space and time. It's funny; I began with many romantic ideas of infinity, and now I longed for, if not a neighborhood, then at least a few streets where I could feel at home. Instead, I found chaos and coldness everywhere. The only thing that wasn't utterly chaotic was my work, but while I was succeeding in it I never considered work a real part of life. Everywhere I turned I felt blocked.

My parents' letters and phone calls were coming farther and farther apart. It was as if, now that I'd achieved economic independence, they felt they were at last independent of me, their strange and almost alien offspring, and could at last "retire" as my parents. Sometimes I didn't even feel that the woman who held the title was actually my mother. I would sit by my bedroom window (which had an extraordinary view of the sky) and try to remember as much as I could about her, such as the time she wiped ice cream off my face. Well, perhaps I had had a mother after all. And a father too, stern and forbidding though he was. Still, they weren't people I could turn to, and I continued to look to my new city for my sense of home.

It wasn't long before I made the mistake of visiting one of the darker pockets of New York—Hell's Kitchen. I thought I might play my game (the hide and seek one) with a prostitute but the results were disastrous, much too painful for me to want to even think about. The prostitutes drove me back to my apartment, as it were, where I could only pace like a caged animal and then sit on my bed staring at the intractable white walls until they fused into a single endless snowbank.

Nothing like a shiver down your spine to make you stand up and do something for yourself. I was still young, with lots of energy and ideas. Obviously I had reached an impasse and it was time to try to think my way out of it. My apartment, like the abominable snowman, had set me off running in the opposite direction. I went downtown by taxi to treat myself to a Saturday lunch at the first good restaurant I saw.

At work we had been trained to analyze products with marketing problems, to come up with scenarios to improve them. I decided it was high time to apply such a critique to myself. I was in SoHo when this happened, far out of my normal route. I was also eating lunch at an odd time, four o'clock, in quite an elegant restaurant on Spring Street. I took a window seat and noticed there was only one other couple eating, a man and a woman in their early fifties. From their snatches of dialogue I judged them to be painters; their harmless but forlorn eyes confirmed my judgment. I ate my chicken crepes and watched people parade by in their leather and furs and cowboy boots and gangster-style hats. Although it was cold, a number of women wore short skirts, their legs gleaming like swords in the street lights. When I finally turned to my left to relax my neck muscles, I noticed a wall-length mirror. At first I turned away, but then gradually I looked at myself. I was very similar to the other men in my department, I concluded, which, given my special needs, might be exactly the problem. I hurried through the rest of my meal so I could spend more time studying myself. Finally I got up from my table and walked toward the mirror to get a closer look.

My appearance had no U.S.P. (unique selling point), that was undeniable. But maybe my imagination could create an alternative. The mirror will not show you the future, that's for sure— not unless you come armed with your imagination. The painter couple now openly watched me as I practiced different walks, and even a kind of dance, in front of the mirror. I didn't care; I can be quirkily unself-conscious, like anyone else. Though I've actually been paralyzed with self-consciousness for most of my life, I also have a capacity to rise to the occasion. I was using the mirror now as a tool to re-create myself. No wonder I was dancing in slow, delicious circles near the end.

I had determined that muscles were crucial to my new appearance, and that the Y was the natural place to develop them. But I soon found that the Y was not the place for me to achieve my new look. There is something about body-builders, would-be or otherwise, that is indescribably repellent. I had thought I would identify with them, but I couldn't. Besides, the awful smells there that brought back memories of the Beachwood bathhouse were much too distressing.

I left the Y after a few sessions and bought the weights and mirror I needed to work out in my living room. After a few months I'd fleshed out my six-foot frame and become quite a menacing figure. As an added touch, I bought a jet-black wig— a savage slicked-down pompadour. Then I found a T-shirt near Times Square that said "The Spirit of New York" in blood-red letters, and I began wearing it underneath my black leather

jacket whenever I went out late at night. I was very unhappy
when the shirt faded, for I never found another like it. Why
hadn't I bought more than one when they existed?

I began walking from my apartment on 105th Street toward
Barnard College. It was a little past midnight, and I could feel
my new muscles rippling like waves, could feel the new blackness
of my hair and jacket. It was the first uniform I'd ever liked.
I thought, If someone from work were to see me, they'd never
recognize me. Not now. I was aware that my simple presence
was probably frightening numerous young coeds. It was a subtle
feeling, but it helped me for my first few blocks.

At 109th Street I saw her walking alone with her head down.
She was tall and thin and stooped a little. She also wore glasses
and had wrapped her blue scarf around herself as tight as a
mummy. Using the parked cars and trees as camouflage, kneel-
ing down and running monkey-like at times, I managed to get
a half-block ahead of her. If she turned now all would be lost,
of course; but I felt that she wouldn't. I moved up one car,
crouching behind a blue Buick, a hydrant, and a clump of skinny
sycamores. She kept walking nearer. At the decisive moment I
emerged and nearly collided with her. She seemed to reel, her
eyes going up in her sockets like Little Orphan Annie's.

"Sorry," I said. "I was checking my tires and didn't see you.
Are you OK?"

She nodded quickly, like a puppet. She couldn't even manage
a word for me she was so frightened. I watched her disappear
into her apartment two doors up, looking back over her shoulder
at me once as I stood firm, like a large rock that had suddenly
materialized on the street.

Then I got another idea. (I hadn't improvised like this since
my days with Michelle.) I walked a few blocks further and
entered the vestibule of another doormanless walk-up. If I
wanted to, I could get in the building quite easily; but that
could be construed as a crime, and I wanted no part of it. I
found a way to curl up as thin as a carrot behind the door and
then suddenly to approach when someone was fumbling with
their key or waiting to be buzzed in.

I got what looked to be an eighteen-year-old undergraduate
that way. Short and confused-looking, he nearly dropped the
books he was holding. Later, in a different building, I had even
more satisfying results. "Oh!" a blond woman with Karen-like
hair gasped, "you frightened me!" I tried to hide my delight as
I apologized. I like it best when someone tells me I've scared
them, without my having to ask first.

Riding the wave of her testimony, and recalling her startled
green eyes and her hair, which seemed to have been swept back
from fright, I arrived home ecstatically happy. Was it the in-
toxication of my sudden pleasure or something else? I still don't
know, but I felt compelled to measure myself. I made a dot on
the wall where my head ended (repeating the process three times)
and discovered that I was now six feet one. I had grown an
inch.

Six feet one, six feet one, I repeated like a mantra whenever
I went out. I had considered buying elevator shoes at one point,
asking myself, Why should my body have grown horizontally
but not vertically? But now it had grown vertically and I had
no explanation for it, which made it all the better.

At the office no one commented on my new height. They
were a perversely jealous group of midgets, and that lack of
reaction was to be expected. I tried to blend in and be one of
them. I was hardworking and conscientious, as I devoted myself
to campaigns to scare people into buying our products. ("I've
fallen and I can't get up" wasn't my line, but it could have been.)
I was essentially a yes man, though I had developed a certain
prickly sense of humor that I occasionally turned on my bosses,
but in a playful enough way that it usually ended up pleasing
them. Except for my muscles, I dressed and looked like everyone
else.

But after work I was as different from them as could be. It
was as if a gate had been opened, and though it was dark out,
I could suddenly see the world. I felt infinitely stronger, yet my
step was lighter, my senses more acute. I could feel my heart
beat and when the action was good, I would sometimes grow
three or four inches taller. I made the amazing discovery (which

I never shared with anybody) that it's not just our genitals that can spontaneously expand or contract.

When it was over and I returned to my height of six one and was back in my apartment, I'd feel let down and I'd take a tranquilizer to ease the transition from so much excitement to the somber world of sleep and the even more somber one of work.

It was a small price to pay. My walks rarely disappointed me. The only bad times were with some of the prostitutes. They were so insensitive and uncaring. Their indifference went beyond "professionalism"; it was zombie-like. If every person is scary in their own way (and I fervently believe they are), prostitutes were scary for being like the living dead. Giving them up, and the orgasms that occasionally went with them, was a minor sacrifice. It was no more difficult, say, than leaving home had proved to be.

When it rained, the action would be slower, but one night I went to the subway and things changed again. The station lay before me like a giant Parcheesi board, but there was a difference. People were constantly angling toward the "safety spaces," though when they got there they discovered those spaces were illusory. Where was there even one safety space? It wasn't too near the track, or on the benches, or by the telephone that rarely worked. It wasn't near anyone else, for everyone else was a stranger, and in the underworld light of the station everyone looked menacing. In the subway it was always Halloween.

In such a world my opportunities multiplied, but so did my anxieties. I didn't want to frighten anyone near the tracks so badly that they might fall, and I didn't want to provoke someone into attacking me, for people have a habit of carrying and using concealed weapons in such places, à la the "subway vigilante" himself. After a ten minute tug-of-war about what to do that ended in a stalemate, a train roared by. I followed its sound and then its gleaming tail until it wound out of sight. Then I turned and saw some action. Usually I focused on solitary people, but a mother and daughter seated on a bench fifty yards from me seemed ideal. They were talking to each other very animatedly, and they were both wearing navy blue, which is one of my favorite colors to scare people in. I circled behind them, walking just in front of the billboards. They were having quite an argument. As their rhetoric intensified, I wondered if they were really a mother and daughter. Perhaps they were lovers instead—I couldn't be sure. I crouched as I approached them (though I could feel myself growing again). Then the younger woman turned to the older and shrieked, "You can't buy love, and if you could you wouldn't spring for it anyway!"

For a second I froze. The words were said with such cruel conviction that I thought the lover/mother might hit her. Instead she said, "You're awful," and turned her head away. I didn't see what happened next, as I was backpedaling on all fours until I could safely stand. A moment later I took an uptown train. While I was riding I thought, That's the most bitter remark I've ever heard. Then I thought it was something I had actually said myself, to one of my parents, but to which one I couldn't be sure. Maybe I had said it to both? Though as time passed, I grew less certain I'd said it at all. Sometimes, at night, my memory would grow and contract like my height.

Still, the fact that I might have said it, or could have said it, wouldn't leave me alone. I'm not going to let that remark torture me anymore, I said to myself as I got off at 110th Street. I don't deserve to be tortured by something I'm not even sure I said, something inflicted on me from the night air of New York.

I saw an older woman in a white uniform, white shoes. A nurse? A waitress? She was standing alone by a pole. I circled behind her quickly, like a pelican searching for fish, so that I could suddenly stand next to her with a dark expression on my face. She gave a little start, a spastic kind of nod. "I'm sorry, did I startle you?" She shook her head. Ah, she was a proud one, this nurse/waitress, but I'd seen what I'd seen and knew what I knew nonetheless. Not even ten minutes later I got two eleven-year-old girls by the same pole my proud nurse had just vacated. They gasped, then turned numb. I apologized in more detail than usual and raced for the next train before anything could happen. The subway had been a success.

My midnight walks got me through the rest of my twenties. Occasionally I would stray from my path and go to the zoo in the afternoon, or to a ballgame, but I felt oddly displaced and it never worked out as well. That's one reason why I stayed away from Port Authority and Penn Station. Crowds depress me in every way. A few times I went back to the flesh markets at 42nd Street; I thought I might find one or two of the girls I knew, but I didn't. What with AIDS scaring everybody two-thirds to death, I was better off staying away from them anyway. There was a whole new cast of zombies now, maybe due to AIDS, but they looked more fearful than ever. There was no point in scaring the already scared, so there was no action there.

Shortly after I turned thirty I made an important contribution to a network campaign for a fast-food restaurant. My promotion to middle management brought me my own office, which was a relief. My boss said, "You're one of us now." I must confess it made me happy. I knew he was inane, but he could make me happy. I knew he spent his life frightening his employees and plotting with them to con people into buying our clients' products; still, his praise made me happy. A paradox, but one I accepted. I won't puzzle over it anymore, I said to myself. I'll celebrate instead. They had actually wanted to take me out to dinner, but as usual I declined, saying I had to take care of my ill mother. (In reality, I hadn't heard from her in weeks.) My greatest accomplishment at the agency had been turning my dread of after-office socializing into an advantage. People said of me: "He has integrity. He doesn't scheme to get ahead by throwing parties or attending dinners." Besides, while no one liked me, no one was jealous of me either. I was regarded as a private man and a workaholic. My boss had even jokingly blessed my compulsiveness once, and that had made me happy too.

I could barely wait until midnight to put on my by now badly faded T-shirt, my wig and leather jacket. I'm treating myself well tonight, I said to myself as I left my building. I had never felt more positive or more powerful as I walked up West End

Avenue. It was an extremely humid spring night. I could scarcely contain my anticipation as the blocks went by without action. Everyone was big or in groups, it seemed, but I refused to be discouraged. Instead, I turned right onto Broadway, heading for the subway at 110th.

It started happening as I walked downstairs, more and more with each step. By the time I reached the platform I was at least six foot eight. As if they'd heard the thunder of my coming and had all fled, the platform was deserted. I went to a dark space under a stairway and waited. I thought, If I keep growing my head will hit the stairway and I'll have to crouch while I wait, or else lie down like one of the homeless. I looked out again on both sides. I was hoping for a woman, of course, but there weren't any.

Finally, someone. Though it was a boy, everything else was right. He was alone with his books, about eighteen years old, with orange strawlike hair long enough to be a girl's. He sat down on a bench about fifty feet to my left and started reading. It would be difficult to circle him, but I wasn't in a circling mood anyway. If I walked right at him, my size alone would do it. At the last moment I'd veer to the right and he'd look up and find himself sitting next to a giant.

I began my walk, aiming myself directly at him. I am a mountain, I thought.

As I suspected, the boy kept his head buried in his book during my entire walk. Then, when I was two feet from him, he stood up unexpectedly and we bumped. He was startled— shocked, in fact—but he said nothing.

"Sorry," I said, but I didn't move. I wanted more acknowledgment of what had happened, so I stood in front of him.

He looked up at me, his face twisted like a corkscrew. "What's your problem?"

"I don't have any problems. Sorry about the collision."

"You walked right into me. I saw you!"

Instinctively, I put my hand over my heart to protest my innocence. At the same time he reached into his pocket and took out a switchblade. For a second we stood stunned, facing each other. Then I went into my monkey crouch, let out a scream and barreled into him, knocking him back into the bench. I punched him hard in the stomach twice, and he gasped and dropped his little knife. His face went white, like he'd been electrocuted.

"Look what you did!" I hissed, shaking my hand in his face.

"Please," he mumbled, petrified.

"Get out of here!" I hissed once more. He turned and ran to the turnstile, squirming through like a fish through a net.

For a minute I began spinning in circles like a top while I shrank down to six one. Then I looked at the platform and saw that what he'd dropped was a pen, a silver ballpoint that I had somehow mistaken for a switchblade. I stared at it, mesmerized, though I never touched it. Finally a train came. I sat in a corner thinking about his pen and the silly line about it being mightier than a sword, which in this case had been strangely true in a way, although also false. When I got to my lobby I shielded myself from my doorman, saying the quickest of hellos. Mercifully, there was no one on the elevator or on my floor.

The first thing I did in my apartment was to take my tranquilizer, wash my hands, and assure myself that nothing terrible had happened. But no sooner did I feel relief than a hideous anxiety swept through me, like the clouds I could see massing outside in the night sky. Just what did I think I was doing? I had hit someone, thus breaking my own anti-violence rule not once but twice. Had I no conscience at all? Then the attorney for my defense (who these days occupies only an equal part of my brain with my prosecutor) rose up and spoke for me: It was an aberration, an incident that had never happened before; and besides, I thought I was acting in self-defense. Anyway, I do nothing compared to what other people do. I don't hurt people in relationships. I don't mug, rob, rape, or pass on diseases. I don't break hearts, faith, or contracts. All I do is scare a series of strangers for a few seconds, and until tonight nothing awful has ever happened.

Then I rememberd Michelle and felt a stab of pain. But that was so long ago; surely I could forgive myself for her by now.

I paced around my apartment alternately reminding myself about my promotion and trying to resolve my dilemma, going back and forth between the rebuttals of my attorney and the accusations of my prosecutor, when suddenly I saw a gigantic white fang in the sky. As soon as I realized it was lightning, I was shaken by a boom of thunder so powerful and penetrating that I instinctively knelt beside my bed for protection. I could feel myself shrinking still more as the horrifying pattern of lightning and thunder persisted, filling my window like a surging white ocean gone amok. I was too terrified to move a muscle. I thought, God is like me. He wants to scare people, so that's why he's doing this.

And still I shook with fear, though for a while I also felt a peculiar sense of mercy for myself.

Psycho in Buckingham Palace

Throughout my adolescence, I secretly yearned for a brother so much that I often thought of my best friends that way. Lester Fischer was the first and most enigmatic of these surrogate brothers.

We met in fifth grade, when my homeroom teacher sat us next to each other. He was new in school, his family having just moved from Dorchester to Brookline, and at first he didn't say a word. But after I told him about the Saturday morning stickball games at the playground, we immediately became friends. In many ways Lester had a perfect playground personality. He was tough but not overly intimidating, funny but not a wise guy, and a good athlete without being a star. He was also smart but not too smart in school.

All through grammar school we spent our afternoons on the playground, usually playing on the same team because we recognized how competitive we each were and wanted to avoid fighting. In the seventh grade we tried out for the school basketball team, and the day we found out we were the starting guards, we screamed for joy. Then, for a minute, before the other players arrived for practice, Lester and I ran around the gym in a delirious circle. It was one of the few truly ecstatic moments of my life, and I think of his, too. I sit in my office now, years later, and wonder how much I'd sacrifice to feel another moment like that. But in those days they seemed possible at any time; in fact, I had another one with Lester a year and a half later.

We went to see *Psycho* on my thirteenth birthday and, like the rest of the audience, shrieked with glee throughout the movie. When it was over we spontaneously hugged each other. From that day on I nicknamed him "Psycho." He was already calling me "Horse" because of a remark our baseball coach had made about my style of running.

I loved being with Lester when he had one of his epiphanies, in part because they seemed so well earned. By nature he was skeptical and sarcastic. He had a sense of black humor before we knew the term for it and a comedian's malleable face with unpredictably intense brown eyes that could express his wildest mood swings. I often thought about his moodiness. I knew he fought a lot with his parents, especially his father, and I decided that must be why he never invited me to his house. He came quite often to mine, however, sometimes to play football in my large backyard that overlooked the school playground, or sometimes to watch a game on TV.

I lived in a white, three-story house with twenty-one rooms, five bathrooms, and four TVs. My parents were both professionally successful and had achieved something of a minor celebrity status in Boston. They did a fair amount of entertaining in the house, but it was still a ridiculous amount of space for our family of three. Lester used to call it "The White House" with a grin that expressed admiration and envy in approximately equal parts. When I saw where he lived I didn't know what to say. He hadn't invited me, but circumstances were such that it was too awkward to leave me waiting on the street.

"Welcome to Buckingham Place," he said with a smirk. It was a small but spotlessly clean apartment, but I was still shocked, having never imagined his home to be so mediocre.

"Where's Ma?" he said, walking into a room without knocking. On the bed sat his sister, whom I had just seen for the first time. She had darker hair and eyes than Lester, and a longer nose. When she saw me she lowered her eyes. "Hey, Retard, didn't you hear me? I brought Ma the clothes from the cleaners."

She got up from the bed and took them from him with a frown. "Oh, by the way, Retard, this is my best friend, Horse.

Horse, this is Bobby, my retarded sister." She barely managed a hello. She was only two years younger but seemed shy enough to be in the fourth grade instead of the seventh. Just before we left the room, however, we exchanged a smile.

One morning, the summer before high school started, from my TV room on the second floor, I saw Lester shooting baskets by himself on the playground. A minute later I was out of my house and crossing Washington Street to join him.

"Psycho," I yelled, as I ran the last fifty yards to the basket. He barely acknowledged me.

"This ball stinks," he said as his jump shot spun in and out. "It's dead. I gotta get a new one." He kept shooting and missing his jump shots without talking or even looking at me.

"So what's the bad news?" I finally said.

"Hold your horses, Horse, I'll get to it."

The bad news was that he was moving. "Now that his life is half over, my old man's suddenly decided he has to have more money and can't make it in Brookline. My mother's really pissed at him."

When I asked him where he was moving, he looked at me with his ironic Humphrey Bogart grin. "Framingham," he said, as he missed a hook shot.

I was shocked again. Although it was only an hour away by bus, no one I knew knew anyone who lived there. He may as well have said Saudi Arabia.

"Look, Horse, don't call me Psycho anymore. That's what I'm calling my old man for ruining my family."

We continued shooting without saying anything for a while. Then Lester said, "Hey, Horse, I know why the ball's dead. It's been shot too many times," and we both started laughing.

As Lester predicted, we didn't see each other much while he lived in Framingham. Occasionally, on vacations or in the summer, I'd reunite with him on the playground, but the rhythm of our relationship had been broken, and neither one of us wanted to risk the effort to try to be as close as we once were.

When my sophomore year in high school ended and my guidance counselor warned that my marks weren't high enough to get into a good college, my parents sent me to an all-boys' boarding school in Groton. With the temptation of girls removed and with strictly supervised evening study hall, my marks improved dramatically. Lester wrote me once in a while from Framingham. Through the constant stream of vitriolic one-liners, I figured out that he was lonely and pretty miserable. His family, however, was apparently prospering. His father's photography business had improved, and his mother was teaching art in a public school, although they were still fighting. Even Bobby had blossomed. "You wouldn't recognize her, Horse. Retard has actually developed some curves. I'll try not to jump her. Naturally, half of Framingham High has the same idea."

He signed the letter "From Lester, Your Brother in Suffering."

The drama of our lives then was twofold: losing our virginity and getting into college. In the spring of my senior year I managed both. I'd slept with a pretty "townie" from Groton, whom I took some serious risks to see, and I'd gotten into Brandeis—possibly with the help of my father who knew someone on the Board of Trustees. As for Lester, he was evasive and contradictory about "the goals," so that my evaluation of his life constantly shifted. Finally he admitted that he'd gotten rejected by all the schools he'd applied to in Boston, but was accepted by Franconia in New Hampshire. It was one of those experimental colleges that sprouted briefly in the middle '60s. I thought I'd miss him terribly, but it didn't turn out that way. College was more exciting than I'd anticipated, and I made lots of new friends in my dorm. Then, in the beginning of my sophomore year, I started going out with Phoebe, the daughter of my creative writing teacher, and a poet and painter herself.

I'd never known a woman as talented as Phoebe or as intensely emotional. She had huge dark eyes like a llama and long black hair that fell down her back. She was a freshman and very babyish in ways, but she had a woman's body, and when we kissed she'd get extremely passionate. I was soon totally immersed with her and realized she was the first woman I'd ever loved. My new emotions amazed me—how easily I could be made jealous, how much I would worry when she was late, how ecstatic she could make me by liking one of my stories—love was all it was advertised as being, only more mysterious. Phoebe herself was full of haunting secrets that obsessed me. How could an eighteen-year-old have lived such a complicated life and have such a contradictory character? She was at once timid and self-effacing and full of the ambition that I associated with men. The effect of all these contradictions was to make me desire her even more.

In the middle of October, Lester wrote me that his parents were getting divorced. He said he "hadn't figured out whose fault it was yet" and that he didn't want to talk about it—ever—until he knew for sure. A month later he dropped out of Franconia and temporarily moved in with his father in Boston. "Psycho is finally trying to be a daddy to me," he explained. Supposedly Lester had a part-time job in Boston, but he soon began spending a lot of time at Brandeis. Of course, I wondered how he'd react to my relationship with Phoebe. I knew that part of him was jealous, but fortunately they got along well and seemed to share a cynical sense of humor that occasionally left me feeling one step behind. The three of us began going out together, and when Phoebe and I went to New York during Christmas vacation, Lester rode beside us on the train. We'd fixed him up with one of Phoebe's friends from N.Y.U. for New Year's Eve. The four of us ended up staying in the same suspicious-looking "hotel suite" in the Lower East Village. That night, which Phoebe had picked to lose her virginity, I had the uncomfortable sensation that Lester had left his date in the adjoining room and had opened our door a crack to spy on us.

All of this unnerved me, of course, but the outlandish was expected from Lester—it was part of the price of knowing him. Somehow I'd tacitly granted him the license—the way a movie audience grants it to a James Dean or Marlon Brando—to act out his emotions the way he needed to. I decided not even to confront him about the eavesdropping. Besides, Phoebe said she thought it was sad, and I didn't want to make him seem even more sympathetic to her.

But the problem didn't go away so easily. One night in February I was with Phoebe in my room in Ridgewood. It was the classiest dorm at Brandeis—all ground level (no stairs to climb) with large picture windows in the rooms. Fifteen minutes after she arrived, we got into bed and started making love. Right in the middle, at the worst moment imaginable, we began hearing loud, repetitive thuds. It took about ten of these thuds before I realized they were coming from the window, and about twenty more before I got up from bed and looked through the blinds. At the top of a little hill in the courtyard, thirty feet away, Lester was making snowballs at a furious pace, making them tight as stones and throwing them at my window as hard as he could. I put some clothes on, opened the door and screamed at him to stop. He fell back into the snow, laughing, while I swore at him and slammed the door. I thought I'd wait him out, but the snowballs continued. If anything, they were harder a half-hour later than they were at first. "I can't believe how immature he is," Phoebe said.

"I can." I was incensed. Finally we got dressed and I called a cab for her. Phoebe lived at home in West Newton with her mother. As soon as she left, I took off after Lester, who was still laughing and screaming obscenities as he ran away from me in the snow across campus.

Lester apologized, claiming he was in love with Phoebe. I accepted his apology but dismissed his claim saying, "You're full of it, I don't want to listen to you."

Eventually I forgave him enough to rarely bring it up, but I did make sure that I talked much less about Phoebe to him. I'd also noticed that Phoebe was proving to be quite flirtatious. Maybe she really did tempt Lester.

Sometime in the spring, Phoebe's mother told us that she had lunch with the editor of a new Boston magazine who wanted to see my fiction and Phoebe's drawings. I shared my elation with Phoebe and began working hard on my story. It's happening, I thought, all my fantasies are going to come true! We'll be like Robert and Clara Schumann, like D. H. and Frieda Lawrence (although I wasn't exactly sure what Frieda had done). A month later the magazine rejected my story but accepted one of Phoebe's drawings. I tried to be happy for her, but I couldn't. Now I was not only jealous of other men, I was jealous of Phoebe herself. The magazine confirmed what I'd suspected anyway: Phoebe was more talented than I was. Her parents were writers, while mine were in business and politics. It was a question of genes, and I was no artist. Just because I wanted to be didn't mean I was.

I withdrew from my creative writing course and started taking courses more appropriate for law school, but it didn't help things with Phoebe. Her flirtatiousness increased as my jealousy did, or maybe I just noticed it more. I stopped spending every weekend with her and began spending more time with Lester. After one such weekend, Phoebe told me in a faltering voice that she'd met someone else, that she wanted out, and was even going to leave Brandeis. Just like that, what I thought would never end was over.

Lester wasn't sympathetic enough. No one was. My parents disappointed me most of all. They adopted the attitude that it was all in the natural course of things, small potatoes compared to what they'd suffered in their lifetimes. I stopped going out with girls and did very little work at school. For months I felt an inexpressible sorrow. One night at Brandeis, after we'd had a couple of drinks, Lester began talking about his family. He described his fights with his father and the way his mother never took his side. Only Bobby could be depended on. We stayed up talking well past midnight. I'd never realized how bad things were with his father, or how much he loved his sister. In my memories Lester was always tyrannizing her. I wondered why he was telling me all this and decided it was his form of sympathy. Toward the end of our conversation I told him he should go back to school.

"No way, Horse. I'm getting too old to be a student. I can't go through the steps, I can't concentrate right."

"That's ridiculous."

"Believe me, I can't cut it. I'm not as intellectual as you."

I felt pleased by his acknowledgment but acted cross with him for neglecting his talent.

After our talk, Lester began spending more time at Brandeis. He was so utterly different from the students there that they were charmed and impressed by him. Because he'd dropped out of college, they thought him a maverick who was truly doing his own thing. Meanwhile, Lester excluded himself from both the Brandeis intelligentsia and the hippies, although he was growing his hair long and combing it forward to cover a premature bald spot. He dressed neatly, but in the same out-of-fashion style he always had. It was strange, but without even trying, he had a gift of fitting in with people. He always talked without pretense, and just when you thought he was trying to be a tough guy he'd wear his heart on his sleeve.

I wasn't surprised that he soon started going out with a senior named Jane Bodowski or "Bodo" as he called her. She was an upper middle-class Jewish girl from Scarsdale, silly and sexy and entranced by Lester's outrageous jokes and behavior.

I tried to feel happy for him, but sometimes I'd catch myself wondering how Lester, who wasn't even a student at Brandeis or anywhere else, could have such an attractive girl while I had no one. Meanwhile, Lester was changing. He started swearing less and smiling more. Even when he told me he was sleeping with her, he did it without any of his usual graphic imagery. In fact, it was clear that he'd only accept so much joking about it. There were changes in his appearance as well. He'd had his hair trimmed and styled, and he began wearing bell bottoms and boots and cotton shirts with bright colors. More important, he'd gotten a job as a salesman at a record store in Harvard Square, and he'd started renting a room on Beacon Street right where Brookline borders on Boston.

Because Bodo was an art major, he began asking me to go to museums with him. Another time he suddenly wanted me to name "the fifty most important symphonies and novels in the world." He started sending away for college applications again and even said he'd begun writing fiction. I encouraged him in all this, of course, but there were times when I envisioned Lester becoming a Nathanael West, while I was pushing papers for a third-rate law firm.

Things didn't happen quite so ironically. I graduated from Brandeis and got accepted by a decent law school. Though not the one I wanted, it still allowed me to stay home. I moved into a one-room apartment a mile from home. The only thing that didn't happen in such an orderly, predictable way was Bodo suddenly breaking up with Lester. I'd pictured them perpetually laughing and dancing to Beatles albums, but faced with life after college, Bodo wanted someone much more conventionally promising. She acted swiftly by getting involved with a medical student in New York a month after she dropped Lester.

Meanwhile, Lester stopped applying to colleges, left his job in the record store, and started driving a cab. That summer he moved into an apartment with Bobby a few blocks from mine. He vowed "to take care of Bodo's little Doc" even if he had to go down to New York to do it. I never fully believed this, as Lester hadn't left Massachusetts for a day ever since he went to New York with Phoebe and me. Eventually he stopped talking revenge but began taking his anger out on Bobby, picking fights with her almost every time I was there.

One night Lester was late from work, and Bobby was fixing supper and half watching TV when I came over. She offered me a beer, and we sat down at the kitchen table to talk for a few minutes.

"I'm really worried about Lester," she said. "He's getting worse lately."

I sipped my beer and answered her nonchalantly, but in my mind something frightening and beautiful was happening. Her big dark eyes, her entire face had fused with Phoebe's, and for a moment I couldn't separate them until, staring more closely, I realized that Bobby had a slightly longer nose.

I changed the subject and began talking to her in a more intimate voice. Bobby followed my lead in the same subtly flattering way I'd identified with Phoebe. I was tremendously excited. After all, she was now almost twenty-two and she'd finished her junior year at college. There shouldn't be any reason why we couldn't have a relationship. Just before Lester returned, Bobby and I looked at each other closely, and I sensed that I could sleep with her.

"Hey, Bobby, what are you doing with Horse? You trying to jump him?"

Bobby blushed before assuming her typically combative role with him. "Dry up, Psycho."

"Hey, don't call me that in front of Horse," he said, his face constricted in what I hoped, but could never be too sure, was only mock rage. "Only Horse can call me Psycho. Why isn't supper ready? Instead of trying to rape the Horse, you should be fixing me food." He started laughing wildly while Bobby, swearing at him under her breath, walked into the kitchen.

That night I was suddenly so fearful of Lester detecting what I was feeling that I didn't try to interfere when he started bullying her. Instead, I called Bobby the next day on some pretext and arranged to see her two more times when Lester was out. The second time I took her back to my apartment and we made love.

From the start, I made her swear that she would never tell Lester, no matter how hard or cleverly he interrogated her. She said she understood and agreed that he could never deal with it. I trusted her, but I was always very careful when I was with the two of them, or even when I was alone with Lester.

Bobby was funny and modest and passionate, but I knew after a month or two that I would never really fall in love with her. Still, I couldn't let her go. For one thing, my last year at law school was more difficult and stressful than I'd imagined, and I was very grateful to have Bobby, who was an unfailingly good listener and who knew how to encourage me. Because Lester was in such despair over Bodo, I felt too guilty to tell him any of my career anxieties, and because my parents were so involved in their own careers, I couldn't talk to them either. I became more dependent on Bobby than ever, even as I yearned for a deeper attraction.

When the pressures in school increased, I began to see Bobby more often at Lester's, and the more often I saw her with him the more I worried that he'd find out.

"Hey, Retard," he said one night when I was over for dinner. "I've got a great idea. Why don't you marry the Horse and then we can all live together. You can cook for both of us, and Horse and me could take turns poking you at night."

"That's hilarious, Lester," she said from the kitchen, where she was washing dishes.

"Horse, you wouldn't care would you?"

I shrugged my shoulders and half smiled. I was trying to show him that I wasn't offended while not encouraging him to go on with his joke. Since he'd learned of Bodo's engagement a month ago, his jokes and temper tantrums had become significantly more vicious. Worse still, I sometimes thought he was mistreating Bobby with one eye on me, to see how I'd react. If I intervened in a serious way, I'd risk revealing my relationship with Bobby and possibly getting into a fight with Lester, whom I was always secretly afraid of. I still had vivid memories of his classic fights on the playground.

"Maybe Horse's parents could rent out the top floor of their palace, and the three of us could live there. Then I could tell Bodo that I live in a palace, and she might visit me and give me some decent sex."

I couldn't tell if the sound that followed was his anger or laughter. A moment later he got up from his chair, saying that he wanted to get some beer. Laughing, he warned us not to do anything funny while he was away.

"I think Lester's flipping out," Bobby said as soon as he was gone. "Yesterday he got drunk so he could call Bodo, and then when she wouldn't speak to him he started taking it out on me."

"What'd he do?"

"He said he was going to write her a letter, but he got mad 'cause he said he couldn't write. He said you should write it for him, that you owed him for all the fun you've had with me. I told him to shut up, that he was crazy, and then he told *me* to write his letter, but I said I wouldn't till he apologized. Then he just threw me down on the floor like I was a bag of groceries. I got up and threw a lamp at him, and he ducked and threw a book back at me. It was like a crazy game of Ping-Pong. He was screaming his head off, and I ran into the kitchen and pulled out a knife."

"A knife?"

"Yeah, a steak knife. He was about five feet in front of me, and I saw his face go white. He called me a lying whore or something and left."

I put my arms around Bobby, who was trembling in spite of her attempt to act tough. We talked about what to do for a couple of minutes, but there wasn't much to say except we should be careful and patient. Then Bobby said she was very sorry to be telling me all this with my bar exam coming up. She asked me how the job interviews were going, and I told her I'd had two in New York.

"Will you wanna go there if they take you?" she said in a shaky voice.

"There's nothing definite yet," I said, turning away from her and looking out their small living room window.

"So, Horse, I hear you're moving to the Big Apple to be a lawyer. Congratulations!" Lester swished his set shot and, for a moment, seemed pleased with himself. We were on the playground on a Saturday morning.

"How'd you know?" I said, a slight edge in my voice.

"Bobby told me. You know she can't keep a secret from me."

My hook shot rattled in and out, and I turned away from him to chase down the ball. "I was gonna tell you today."

He shrugged, as if to say it made no difference.

"She's gonna miss you. The little sis is really fond of you."

"I'll miss her too. Come to think of it, I'll even miss you, you crazy bastard."

Lester blushed as he always did when he was flattered.

"We'll have a party for you at our place, Horse, invite some of the guys over, OK?"

"Wait, I've got a better idea. My parents are going away to a convention so we can have it in my house next week. We'll have much more space, and I'll invite plenty of girls, so you'd better be in a good mood."

Lester smiled thinly. "I'll try" he said, just before his jump shot rolled off the rim.

Not many people showed up for my farewell party. Three years had passed since my class had graduated from college, and many of the people I was friendly with had already moved. Since I'd gotten my job—a good starting position in a reputable New York firm—I, too, longed to leave Boston. I was sick of its academics and provinciality. I felt Bostoned to death and longed for New York's expansiveness.

I told Lester I was having touble getting girls to come to the party, but he hardly seemed to care. He'd decided to make an all-out effort to persuade Bodo to come—even offering to pay her airfare from New York. Bobby and I shook our heads at his deluded tenacity, but a few days later I began fantasizing about inviting Phoebe. When I finally reached her in Vermont, I ended the conversation in a few minutes without mentioning the party. A man had answered the phone.

Things are ending neatly, I remember thinking. Bobby remained something of a problem, but I thought our relationship would just melt away and that eventually she'd become a good friend. I imagined that during dinner one night, when we were all married, she and I would tell Lester about our affair, and we'd all laugh about it.

I couldn't have thrown the party without Bobby. She took me shopping a few hours before the party, or rather I gave her all my money, and she picked out the right food and liquor and managed to give me $150 change when we got back. "You still don't have a wallet," she said as I stuffed the money in my pockets. "Don't you think you should get one before you go to New York?"

I didn't want to see the expression on her face, so I laughed and ran upstairs and put the money in my bureau drawer the same as when I was a child.

For some reason I felt enormously attracted to Bobby that day, but even though she'd never been in my parents' house before, I couldn't entice her to take a tour until she'd finished her preparations for the party. When she was finally done, I was so excited I started undressing her while we walked upstairs. At the top of the stairs we kissed and I noticed her eyes were moist and wide open—so large and beautiful I didn't think to look down at her nose as I usually did.

We started making love in my father's room, continued in my mother's room, and ended in my bedroom, which was still kept as it had been when I lived there seven years before. Afterward, I held and kissed her much longer than I usually did and only stopped when I heard someone knocking on the back door that led into the kitchen. "It's Lester, get dressed," I said as I ran downstairs.

When I opened the door, our eyes met for a second before he looked down at the floor.

"I'm a dead man."

"What happened?"

"Bodo ain't coming. She's really gonna marry that fag."

"I'll get you a drink."

"Where's Bobby? She here?"

"She's upstairs cleaning. She came over early to help fix things up."

"Hey, Horse, you ain't drilling her, are you?" I laughed at his choice of words. Every month he called sexual intercourse by a different term.

"Sure I am. Every day, and your mother on weekends."

Our eyes met and he smiled.

"Get me another gin."

Despite Bobby's elaborate preparations and a house with three floors, the party didn't click. There weren't enough people to justify moving to another floor, so for the most part people stayed in the living room. Also, some of the guests hadn't seen each other in three or four years, and that was proving more awkward than I'd anticipated.

Bobby and I had agreed not to dance with each other. The few times I talked with her, she seemed depressed and out of place. When she did dance, I'd feel a stab of jealousy, and I'd want to make love with her again. Why am I leaving this woman, I said to myself, who is the sweetest and best I've ever known? Why, when I go to New York in a week, don't I take her with me? Is it really something as trivial and ridiculous as the size of her nose? Of course not, I answered myself in my newly certified attorney's voice. She's neither intellectually nor socially sophisticated enough, make that challenging enough. You could have a decent life with her, but it would be a limiting one, one that would never be dynamic enough to develop your own potentialities. She is sweet as Brookline is sweet, but you're leaving for a new world in a week. Better to let Bobby and Brookline both melt away.

About an hour after the party began, Lester started drinking by himself in a corner of the living room. When I tried to cheer him up, he muttered something I couldn't understand and walked into the kitchen. I let a half-hour go by, watching the few couples who were dancing under the chandeliers to "Sympathy for the Devil" or to "Reach Out." Bobby was dancing with the guy who used to play forward on my grammar school basketball team. I walked into the kitchen and saw Lester sitting at the table, holding a glass of vodka.

"What's going on?"

"I didn't want to ruin your party so I came in here."

"Is it Bodo?"

He nodded.

"But you knew she wasn't going to come to this. I mean, she lives in New York."

"You don't understand, Horse. She's gonna marry that little fag. Not that I blame her. Face facts: I drive a cab. If you were marrying someone, who would you want, a surgeon or a cab driver? Don't answer. Your parents make more than two surgeons put together."

He finished his drink and poured himself another. He drank a lot that night and talked longer and more bitterly than I ever remembered. After another hour or so, Bobby appeared in the doorway, but I signaled her to leave us alone, and she left along with the other guests a little later.

Nobody escaped Lester's wrath that night. He began railing against his father and mother, then against his high school and grammar school teachers, then at Bodo. "Even Bobby stabbed me in the back," he said, staring right at me. My heart skipped a beat, but I returned his stare and said nothing.

"That's right, say nothing. You're too rich to have to worry about who you stab and who you don't anyway. You've lived your whole life like a prince in a palace, and now you're going to move to New York like Bodo, the Queen of Scarsdale. You never knew what it was like to have to worry about money, to have your whole family worry about it. That's why you did better than me in school, and that's why you got more ass, too. In the end, they always go where the money is."

I let it pass. I felt sorry for him, and a little worried.

"If it's any consolation to you, I don't have a girlfriend now, and I assure you I'm not happy."

"You don't, huh? Well, you will!" he said, staring at me in an accusing way. "You're gonna make big bucks and own a summer house and marry a beautiful piece. You'll have it all, and you'll forget about your old friends, too."

When he started to sober up later, he turned apologetic, with genuine sorrow in his voice. I told him to forget it, that I understood, and asked him if he wanted to stay over. I think I said he was in no condition to go home.

"You can stay in my room," I said. He mumbled a thank you and followed me upstairs. I told him we could talk in the morning if he wanted to, and I went to my father's room, where I hadn't slept since I was a child.

When I woke up, I lay in bed for a while reviewing the events of the night before. Then I went downstairs and fixed myself breakfast. I ate slowly, reading the newspaper thoroughly, but there was no sign of Lester. I climbed the stairs, calling out his name a couple of times on the way up. Lester was right, I thought, as I checked the den and then the TV room, this place is obscenely large. "Lester," I said, as I walked into the music room. No one was there either. The door to my room was open. I saw a set of keys I'd given him on my desk that faced an enormous copper beech tree outside my window, but there was no note next to it. A shudder ran through me as I opened my bureau drawer. The money that I'd gotten back from shopping with Bobby the day before was missing, all $150.

I searched through the drawers, although I knew very well I'd hidden it under my socks in the top drawer. Then I kicked my bureau and swore and pounded my walls. It was Lester, I knew it, although it wouldn't be fair even to accuse him unless I was sure. I tried to think of a possible scenario that could explain it and imagined he might have taken a cab to Logan Airport and flown straight to New York to see Bodo. Perhaps he planned to pay me back as soon as he returned. I went to my address book and a moment later was talking to Bodo on the phone.

No, she hadn't heard from Lester since yesterday afternoon when she told him that she wasn't coming to the party, but what a nice surprise to hear from me. How was the party, how was Brookline? We were such good friends at college, and now that I was moving to the city we should have a drink sometime and reminisce.

When I got off the phone I wanted to take a walk, but I was afraid to leave the house. Instead, I began to analyze everything that had happened. I could construct a chronology of events, but when I tried to account for motives I found myself pacing aimlessly around the house. Finally I called Bobby and told her about the money.

"Don't worry," she said. "I'll find out if he did it. I know where he is."

"How can you find out?"

"I know how to get it out of him."

"Call me as soon as you know, OK? I feel horrible suspecting him if I'm not right."

"Of course," she said softly.

I drank part of a beer left over from the party and thought about what Bobby said. Then I ran upstairs to the TV room. My premonition was correct. Lester was shooting baskets by himself, looking over his shoulder at my house after every third shot. I jerked my head away from the half-raised shade. His meaning was obvious. If you've got something to say to me, come down and say it one on one, where I'm waiting for you, where I've always been—on the playground. I was furious but also worried. I decided to wait. I couldn't do anything till I knew he took the money anyway.

A minute later I began watching him again. He went through the same routine: jump shot, set shot, hook shot, then a look up at my house. This time it seemed our eyes nearly met, though I was only looking through two inches of the window. I felt repulsed but mesmerized and found myself going through my own routine of watching, then turning away every time he turned around to look up at me.

Then I saw Bobby in her leather jacket and tight jeans walking toward Lester. He kept shooting as if he didn't notice her until she got right next to him. I turned away. I suddenly felt tired and lay down on my mother's bed and half slept while I waited.

An hour later, Bobby called.

"He took it, all right. I'm really sorry."

"How'd he tell you?"

"At first he denied it, but I knew he was lying, he wouldn't even look at me. I said, 'How could you do that to him after he's been your best friend all these years?' Then he finally looked at me and screamed, 'And how could you sleep with him, you little whore! You're a great one to talk.' I said he didn't know what he was talking about, but he said he knew I was lying. He said, 'Horse took from me first when he wanted to, so I took from him. I needed the money.' I told him his analogy stunk, that if we didn't tell him, it was to spare his feelings. He looked sad for a second. Then he turned his head away and said you were his best friend and that he'd pay back the money and that he felt like killing himself. He also said he knew you'd never forgive him.

"So that's the story. I'm really sorry. Can I still see you before you go?"

"Of course, I'll call you in a couple of days."

"You don't hate me for telling him, do you?" I felt a little surge of anger that I managed to suppress.

"I don't hate anyone. I feel sad, that's all. I'll speak to you soon." I tried to convince myself that I meant what I said, but a minute later I knew Lester was right. Our long friendship, as well as my shorter one with his sister, had come to an end.

Some of the things that Lester prophesied for my life came true, but typically in ironic ways. I survived and got promoted at the firm, but I never liked my work and remained afraid of my superiors. I grew to enjoy my apartment on the Upper East Side, but I never married and, despite a succession of girlfriends, often felt lonely or disappointed.

A month after his theft, Lester sent me a short letter of apology with $15 crumpled up in the middle of it. "Here's my first installment. I won't ask you to forgive me till I'm all paid up. I'll be sorry for this my whole life. Lester."

I almost called him but instead I waited. Eventually he phoned me a couple of times from Brookline, swearing he'd pay me back (I sensed both times that he'd been drinking). I told him that I wasn't mad at him anymore, that I understood, but I couldn't say any more than that. After two months I realized there'd be no more installments or phone calls.

A few days after my last conversation with Lester, Bobo called and invited me to meet her for a drink in the Village. At the bar she told me that she'd broken her engagement with the doctor (who was actually becoming a chiropractor), although she was still seeing him. Neither of them was really sure they wanted a complete commitment, and they'd both decided to keep their relationship open. She added that she hoped this wouldn't get back to Lester as she had no desire ever to see him again. I could tell from the look in her eyes that she knew what would happen next. Almost automatically, we went back to her apartment and had sex in the perfunctorily kinky style of the day.

Without talking about it much, we'd have a similar date every month or two. Maybe we liked seeing each other because we both wanted to talk about Lester. The last time I saw her, however, she had a different reaction. I asked her a question about Lester and she said, "I'm sick of talking about him with you. Let's find a different subject." Then she got out of bed and walked to the bathroom, slamming the door behind her.

I heard water running and guessed she was taking one of her long bubble baths. I wanted to leave, but I also didn't want to face my empty apartment, nor could I bear the thought of going back to the office.

Maybe it was the sound of the water—I don't know—but I closed my eyes and started to think a little philosophically. I thought how time is long enough to forget almost everything but short enough to always be wanting something. Though it had been five years since I'd seen him, I started to have a series of memories about Lester. I saw him on the train to New York watching me and Phoebe; I heard him say, "Welcome to Buckingham Palace," with his sad grin in place just before I saw his apartment; I saw him dancing in ecstasy with me around the gym, and then hugging me right after we finished seeing "Psycho."

"Let's make love," said a voice in a whisper. A pair of hands covered my eyes. It was Bodo, who'd returned to bed. She was embracing me, but I kept my eyes closed tight. For another moment I was still inside the movie theater being hugged by Lester.

Rats

I can't remember a moment of my life when I wasn't afraid of something. Early on I realized you're not supposed to talk about such things—nobody loves a worrywart or a coward—so I learned to camouflage it. I willed myself, I think, to be normal looking (some might say pretty, in an unobtrusive way), to never twitch or stutter, to menstruate fairly regularly, and to get an average number of colds per year, though I admit I'm probably what you'd call a hypochondriac. I can also function in most social situations. Occasionally I work behind a cash register at a video store in Harvard Square, for which I also do bookkeeping. Only late at night in my apartment—where I pay a little extra to be in a well-protected building—does any "objective" symptom of my fear show, but then there's rarely anyone to witness it. I'm an incurable insomniac who doesn't even try to sleep in a normal way. Moreover, I'm philosophically opposed to sleep. Here's why.

I can understand that people shouldn't complain too much about their health, that you mustn't give in to your fear of flying or of getting hit by a car or another person, that you must assume you're not getting poisoned when you eat food or swallow an aspirin and, of course, you don't ruin a date by talking about AIDS. But I've never understood how people can lie down in the dark and close their eyes, confidently awaiting sleep. I think I have a very good reason for considering this a lunatic act. Isn't our chief weapon as human beings our alertness? Yet sleeping means dulling your senses, cutting off your alarm system, making yourself the easiest possible prey as you lie blind and helpless in the dark. Instead of this ritual, I follow my own. I take a mild tranquilizer (so I can maintain my basic alertness level and not risk becoming a drug addict) and sit in my armchair and watch TV with the sound off. During this time I'm fully clothed and have the telephone by my chair. One other thing to confess about this: I keep a gun wedged between the cushion and the right arm of my chair. In this way I can get little bursts of "sleep" throughout the night.

Needless to say, the very few men I've had over at night were confused about this. Now that I'm being so recklessly honest, I'll also admit that one of the main reasons I've even had sex is because I was afraid not to. I'm sure this is true for many other people too. Society just makes you feel so freakish if you don't, that you finally do it. I don't deny that sex can feel good and is a pretty powerful instinct, but it's also a greatly overrated one, not nearly as strong as hunger or sleep. I see it as one of the shorter-lasting diversions from serious fear, like drugs or playing sports or eating, as opposed to the longer-lasting ones like television, sleep, work, and relationships in general. Sometimes in my mind I see human life as a giant pharmacy where people perpetually busy themselves selecting their daily menu of distractions. In the pharmacy they decide, "Today I'll eat, take a pill, work, eat, work, drink, eat, go to the movies, have sex, take a sleeping pill, watch TV, and sleep. Tomorrow I'll . . . etc." I told some of this to Kevin who works at the video store with me and he just laughed like I was kidding or was trying to be cute. Kevin, of course, is a perfect example of this. He loves violent movies and sports and all kinds of competitions. He's also very much into his routines. Still, I don't want to give the wrong impression, since Kevin can be extraordinarily sweet and considerate. Also, I have to give him credit for being adventurous enough to ask me out. I guess I'm always surprised when someone takes a romantic interest in me because even though I camouflage my problems very carefully I keep thinking that enough of my true self seeps through to scare men off. An actual date is a genuine shock to me. With Kevin it was so far from my mind (although I always liked his blue eyes, which are amazingly sincere looking, like a child's) that I was able to kind of relax and kid around a lot when I talked to him at work. So when he asked me to the movies I took it as a strictly platonic gesture, figuring he was between girlfriends and just didn't want to go alone. Even when he kissed me goodnight, half on the lips and half on the cheek, I figured he meant it to be a friendship kiss and just missed a little.

Three days later he asked me to go to a Red Sox game and I thought that proved he was just thinking of me as a buddy. It was such a rah-rah thing to do. Also, of course, crowds frighten me but I went anyway, figuring his best friend was sick or busy or heavily involved with a woman. I worked out some pretty elaborate scenarios to cover each of the possibilities. But when he started touching my hair while we were in a bar in Kenmore Square after the game, I had to face what might happen. Then on our third date we went back to my place (he said his was way too messy) and we started making out. I discovered that besides having a nice kissing technique, Kevin was also perceptive in a way. After fifteen minutes of kissing he said he wanted to have sex, and even though I always feel my will drain away at such moments—since I fear doing it or not doing it about equally—and my willingness has historically been interpreted to mean yes, Kevin sensed my indecisiveness (I was also trembling a little) and said, "What's the matter?" I said, "Don't you think this is kind of scary in a way?" and he said, "There's nothing to worry about," and I said, "Well, there's all those diseases for starters."

"No problem, I brought something. Haven't you heard of safe sex?" So finally he said it, with a smile of course—the misnomer of the century, as if sex could ever be safe or bring safety. Still, I took the hint and shut up and let him have sex with me. Later, though, I couldn't resist asking him if there was *anything* he was afraid of.

"I'm not crazy about rats," he said. I laughed because I've always found it funny whenever people single out something and say, "I'm afraid of rats, or heights, or snakes."

"Kevin, my point is the whole *world* is rats." That made him shake his head and force a laugh himself. When he was through he looked at me with something like sympathy in his eyes.

"Ruthie, if you really feel that way, how do you keep from going crazy?"

"I get by," I said. I wanted to say, "I don't. I expect it all to end at any moment."

Incidentally, I have some "objectively" valid reasons for thinking this, since my father died suddenly of a heart attack when he was forty and I was eleven. Though my mother still lives on, as does my older sister, they're so different from me I don't think they could have influenced me much. Anyway, even before my father died I'd developed my sense of danger (it's why I never learned to drive, for instance, and why I stay away from boats and planes), though his death certainly helped convince me. It sounds so grandiose to say you know you're going to die, but many people my age don't. Kevin doesn't seem to know, so even though he's a couple years older I think of him as very young and innocent, which probably helps me pity him and give in to him a lot.

For instance, I assumed that after Kevin slept with me he wouldn't ask me out again or at least would back off. I not only assumed it, I hoped it would happen. It wasn't that I didn't like him or that he'd done anything wrong, it's just that I couldn't imagine the mental pressure of these dates on a regular basis.

Human beings are frightening things. Why? Because they can get angry and hurt so many different ways, so easily. You can blink and offend a human being. Heaven forbid if you should yawn. But if you're on a date with one, they get offended ten times as easily, and if you add to that the fact that they can overpower you physically it's a pretty scary scenario. My way of dealing with it is never to criticize a man or even try to get my own way. The problem with that is I have a brain too, and if I never say what I think my own anger builds up and I can't even get the "bursts" of sleep I'm used to. Instead I might end up throwing things around my apartment after they've left (I'm a great one for practicing random violence on kitchen utensils) or else just crying in my chair and shaking for hours, trapped in my own little emotional earthquake. As if all this isn't enough (and it is, it's more than enough), if you should ever start to like someone your temptation to say what you think, to sing your own personal note, gets twenty times stronger.

Last night, for example, Kevin wanted to stay over. This meant a night of suffering for me, since I'd have to stay next to him in the dark until he fell asleep. I lay in bed with my eyes open, trying to focus on my ceiling to feel a sense of limits and not feel unhinged and just drifting in space as I often do. I felt like I spent nine years in Hell waiting for him to fall asleep. Then, when I thought it was safe, I left the bed, put my clothes on, and tiptoed to my chair. I had started watching what looked like a spy movie (with the sound off, of course) when Kevin suddenly appeared beside me.

"What's up?" he said. I was startled and my heart thumped. It's lucky I didn't reach for the gun. I was also so embarrassed that I started to cry.

"Hey, Ruthie, calm down," he said, putting a hand on my shoulder. He said it so genuinely, I could imagine his blue eyes looking concerned, and that made me cry even harder. Also, I was having what I call an "anxiety blockade," which means so many conflicting anxieties had converged in me that I couldn't do anything except cry. It was like the wall of marbles that would form in the middle of the Chinese checker board when I used to play with my father (each of us playing the marbles for two other imaginary players) and it would suddenly seem that movement was impossible.

I was stuck. I didn't know if I should lie about why I was watching TV or tell the truth. I also didn't know if I wanted Kevin to leave or stay, which was amazing in a way, since the other times I had always wanted the men to go right after it ended. In the past, whenever I used to feel this tug-of-war in my mind I'd try to fight out of it with a compromise. I'd been worrying a lot, for example, about someone breaking into my apartment, so I had bought the gun. But I was also afraid it might go off by accident, making me kill the potential robber/

rapist or even myself. I also worried that said robber/rapist might get the gun away from me and use it on me. My solution was to get a gun but never to keep it loaded. Not wholly satisfying, I admit, but a compromise. This time my compromise-making mechanism wasn't working, and all I could do was cry while poor Kevin tried to pacify me. Finally I told him a short version of why I was sitting in the chair.

"That's understandable," he said. "It's hard to sleep next to someone the first time. I'll bet if you had another drink you could fall asleep real easy."

"You don't understand. I never sleep. I don't believe in it, so I don't even try. I watch TV instead of sleeping."

A strange look came into his eyes. I realize now that I should have just shut up, but instead I started telling him how I was afraid of insects and animals and the greenhouse effect (can't even enjoy a warm day anymore), flying and AIDS and getting fired and having children and not having children and chipping my teeth, and heights and nuclear bombs and parties, and being with people in general.

"Stop it!" he said. "Why are you acting crazy like this? You're not like this."

"Yes, I am. And I'm not acting. I think everyone else is acting by pretending not to be afraid. And I don't think I'm crazy, either. Don't you ever think it's odd that we're the only species in the world that knows we can die at any given second? Doesn't that strike you as kind of an enigma?"

The wounded look returned to his eyes and I knew that he wanted to leave. "People can't live that way," he said softly. Again, an obvious cue to stop, but I couldn't. Instead, I went on and on while I could sense his face turning sour and almost hear the escape lines he was rehearsing in his head.

When he finally did leave he was very sweet, though of course he didn't ask me out again. He told me that I'd feel better in the morning, that I should call him tomorrow if I still felt this bad, that I probably shouldn't drink so much (I'd only had one and a half glasses of wine), that he'd see me at work Monday morning.

Now here's the strangest part of the story. After he left, I watched him through my peephole as he waited for the elevator in the hallway. I could picture its doors closing over him like a shark's mouth. It was a typically gruesome thing for me to think, and I turned away from the door fully expecting to go to my chair. Only I didn't go. My mind was suddenly flooded with images of Kevin toasting me in the Greek restaurant he took me to, then later focusing so intently on me as he unzipped my dress, and then the wounded look in the half dark after I "talked crazy." I started to feel dizzy and my heart began to hurt, so I lay down on my bed. His smell was everywhere—in the sheets, on the pillow, even on my skin. Yet for a moment I felt better. I even closed my eyes and felt the darkness close over me like a black blanket without any images except Kevin's smile. Then the miracle happened: I fell asleep.

When I woke up six hours later (six hours!) my mind was racing. I thought I'd probably pace around my apartment for an hour trying to figure out if I'd really slept or not, but I knew I had. The images of Kevin came back too, and I didn't know whether to laugh or cry or whether I was glad they were back or not.

Life is certainly terrifying, but it can be even more surprising. I ran to the window and stuck my head out. The sun exploded at me like a bomb, but it felt good on my face. The sky was shockingly blue. It was the first time I'd opened my window since I moved in last year. I remember breathing deeply once, twice. I looked down but I didn't feel dizzy. For a while I kept my eyes fixed on Massachusetts Avenue where Kevin had left me to go home last night and I thought, "At long last, you crazy bitch, you've finally experienced something."

Silver Screen

The Ambassador was part of a complex of architecturally indistinguishable condominiums each with a British-sounding title
like Buckingham or Lancaster. When Allen finally arrived it was
nine o'clock, and except for the distant strain of a polka coming
from the recreation hall perhaps a hundred feet beyond the
floodlit swimming pool, silence had settled over the entire
complex.

It was his first visit to his mother since his father's funeral
six months ago, and he'd postponed it for weeks. On the plane
to Tampa he'd reasoned that he was older and more independent
now, that there was no reason for old patterns to reassert themselves. But from the moment she let him in the door and said,
"Are you afraid to kiss you own mother now?" he felt a familiar,
barely containable rage surging inside him.

Before he'd even sat down she began her catalog of medical
problems and moved from there to a detailed description of her
"hellish loneliness." Only by exaggerating the length of his bus
trip from Tampa to Bayside was he able to excuse himself early,
but once in his father's room there were other torments to con-
tend with. His father's clothes were still in the closet. Plaques
and citations celebrating his academic and professional life still
hung on the walls. His mother hadn't removed a thing. Allen
started to give way to the feeling he'd had most of his twenty-
seven years, that nothing was real in the world except his parents, that other people were not fully alive or didn't deserve to
be. It was a kind of inner conviction that everyone he'd met,

everything that had happened to him was somehow counterfeit. Even his suffering was illusory. How could he imagine that he suffered when his mother had hammertoes from arthritis, cysts on her breasts, high blood pressure, and excruciating neck and back aches? And now, since his father's death, his right to suffer was less legitimate than ever. Worst of all, there was no one who could convincingly take his side. His sister might have been an ally, but since his father's death she'd turned reclusive and seemed angry whenever he telephoned, as if he were intruding on her private meditations.

He dreaded lying down in his father's bed and drank a glass of wine to help himself sleep. That night he dreamed he found his father's body buried in the sand. He tried to kiss him back to life and woke up with tears in his startled green eyes.

It was in the Ambassador swimming pool late the next morning that he had his first argument with his mother. She'd told him he had to put on a shirt and shoes before he entered the pool area. He made a sarcastic remark about her "paranoia" but complied. When she was ready for her swim she motioned him toward a shower near the adjoining shuffleboard courts.

"Everyone has to shower before they go in the pool," she said, addressing him as if he were a child.

"That's ridiculous."

"It's a good rule. I don't want to swim in other people's sweat and germs."

The argument escalated rapidly. He accused her of being in love with rules, while she noted that he'd do better to follow more of them. A couple of sentences later his father was invoked as the ultimate example of decorum. Here Allen retreated. He rarely challenged the mythic status his mother and sister afforded his father; indeed, he had grown up idolizing him himself. But he had to resist his mother's attempts to assume the same position in his eyes. He looked at her as she breast-stroked silently past him in the pool. She was sixty-three, but he felt she was still beautiful. That she deified his father was understandable and even touched him. But if it had all been so wonderful, why had they slept for so many years in separate rooms? Was this distance the price they had to pay for their "spiritually profound" relationship? And why did he feel she treated him more like a jealous lover than a son?

He remembered that the few times he'd dared to bring a girlfriend home his mother acted as if her soul were being attacked by a large and brutal army. She immediately set out to reduce the girl's ego to shreds. It would begin with an absurd height contest (this had happened with three different women) that he would have to judge in the living room. Who was taller, his mother or the astonished and frightened young woman who was standing (slouching) next to her? After the contest she'd begin a monologue about her achievements as an English teacher, continue with the standard homage to her husband, and conclude with a mortifying series of allusions to the various important people in her social circle. With a bewildered sense of outrage he would yearn for someone to stop it, or at least to witness it so he wouldn't think later that he'd somehow imagined it all. His father, however, would invariably be at work, and his sister would have discreetly retired to her room to study, or else taken a walk.

Later his mother would locate exactly what he feared most about the girl in question. "Is she really as docile as she seems? Is she really that devoted to you? I think she's terribly ambitious, did you notice? I'll bet that one's a real gold digger. I hope she doesn't think you're rich just because your father's a judge and owns a condominium."

He dove underwater resolving to forgive her because, of course, she needed him, and this latest dispute was merely a trifle. Besides, to his dismay he remembered that he needed to ask her for some money.

Without their ever saying it, Allen knew that both of his parents had wanted him to go to law school in New York and for a while he, too, thought this was what he wanted. But before he'd finished his first year he found it both intimidating and boring and was convinced he'd made a terrible mistake. A long series of arguments with his parents began which was only settled by his agreeing to finish another year at school. At the end of his second year, he'd already managed to get accepted by a business school in Philadelphia. It seemed to him that many of the same skills used in law could be used more creatively, and less hypocritically, in business. If he was going to push papers for a corporation, why not do it for his own? Although he hadn't formulated it exactly this way, he also felt that while he could never equal his father at law, given a fair chance he could out-earn him through business. He had been making a number of valuable contacts with some ambitious young businessmen who'd offered him a quarter-share in a condominium in Wilmington. After his father died, he thought he'd have the $10,000 to buy in, and he asked his friends to wait a while. But his father had left everything to his mother. Now he had another chance to buy into a different condominium with this group for about the same price. At some point during his visit he wanted to speak to his mother about this, but he knew he had to be very careful how he phrased things.

A few minutes later he swam next to her and said he was sorry, then braced himself for the consequences of such an unqualified apology. Usually she'd use it as an occasion to launch into a lament so long and intense that he'd start fighting with her again. This time he forced himself to stay quiet while she talked, diverting himself by looking at the people around the pool—men in their seventies with skin like tired rubber hanging on their stomachs, or sometimes drawn unnaturally tight like stretched parchment. They lay back behind sunglasses in their chaise longues next to their mute wives. Some were playing transistor radios, but no one talked. Everyone seemed to be staring at him because he was new and young, a variation on the scene that had by now anesthetized them. In the end they only served to make his father seem that much more dynamic, remarkable, superbly alive. Implicit in his mother's every remark was a comparison between these benumbed retirees and her husband, who had been active until the moment of his stroke.

After their swim, when they had finally made up, his mother fixed lunch. They sat down to eat, she in one of her bright pink afternoon dresses, he in a green sportshirt and white chinos, by the picture window overlooking the bay. She'd just finished describing her recent operation to remove "a new, suspicious-looking cyst" when she caught him off guard by asking him about his job at the department store where he was an assistant manager.

"So tell me, do you think you'll still have your position next year?"

"It depends on the economy."

"I don't understand an answer like that."

"What's there to not understand? Don't you read the newspapers, don't you watch the news? Bsuinesses are failing left and right. They hire people according to their budgets. If they don't have the money, they can't hire you."

"Your store might go out of business?" she said, raising her thin, penciled eyebrows. "Why do you choose shaky places like that?"

"It's the best I can get, Mother. I choose very little in my life."

"I'll never know why you didn't finish your law degree. Your father begged you, he foresaw."

"Never mind what he foresaw," Allen said, turning away from his mother's tortured stare to look out the window. A crane was flying low over the water, looking for fish. "Did he foresee what's happened to the wonderful economic system he loved to defend?"

"That's a poor excuse. When are you going to stop making excuses?"

"I'm not making excuses. I'm trying to upgrade myself all the time, believe me."

"What do you mean 'upgrade'?"

"For instance, I have a great opportunity to become a partner in a very bright group that's buying condominiums in Delaware."

"Condominiums cost money," she said sharply, cutting him off. "Where do you expect to get that kind of money?"

He looked down at his untouched tuna sandwich. "It's impossible to talk about this with you, isn't it?"

"You want more money from me?" she said, pointing her knife at her chest as if he were stabbing her. "Six months after your father's buried, when I don't know how I have the strength to get up each morning, you want to talk to me about condominiums?"

"Forget I mentioned it." They were silent for a minute. He pretended to look out the window, but to his relief he saw that her eyes were softening.

"Listen, if you can't get a job you always have a home here, you can always come here," she said.

This wasn't what he'd hoped to hear, and he felt tricked and humiliated. "I'd rather be dead," he said softly, getting up from the table and walking back to his father's room.

A half-hour later his anger turned to guilt and he knocked softly on his mother's door. She ignored him. This too was a ritual between them, and he knew he would have to begin apologizing convincingly through the door. But his mother resisted his initial peace offering. There were some things she wanted to say to him first.

"You come here on practically the eve of your father's funeral and all you want to do is worm some money out of me."

"I wasn't trying to worm anything—" he protested.

"That's all I am to you, a checking account, a cash register, so you can spend it all on some gold digger who doesn't care a damn about you—"

"That's not true—"

"I offer you my home and instead of thanking me you want some money to spend on whores—"

"That's a lie!" he screamed. He began swearing at her, a long medley of curses said with a strange facility. When it was over, he walked across the living room and then directly down the hallway and out the door. On the way to the elevator he nearly bumped into an old man in flip-flops returning from the swimming pool. The man (who seemed unusually tall, perhaps because his neck was so long) was so surprised by the near collision that his watery blue eyes appeared to double in size. Allen, apologizing hastily, ran down the stairs instead of taking the elevator.

Only when he decided to walk toward the beach did he realize the enormity of the complex. He saw it in a succession of planes laid out one after the other in a stupefying geometry — the plane of the parking lot, then the plane of the shuffleboard courts, behind that the tennis courts, then the swimming pool, and finally the recreation hall where there were weekly dances. Everywhere there were lines and arrows and signs designating which areas belonged to which condominiums. The condominiums, were spread out in parallel planes of their own.

Still trembling with anger and repeating in his mind the insults he and his mother had exchanged a few minutes before, he took a shortcut past the Ambassador tennis court, where an old man wearing a floppy white tennis hat was reaching in vain to return his grandson's modest forehands. Invariably when he saw such scenes he was reminded of how he'd never played any sports with his father. His father had tacitly communicated that sports were frivolous, and that overindulgence in them was criminal. A mere raising of his eyebrow after Allen returned from playing basketball at the schoolyard could communicate infinite disdain. But for all his sternness and air of authority, his father had never even raised his voice at him. (That was left to his mother.) In everything he did, his father's behavior was technically irreproachable but elusive, faintly detached. After he died Allen felt a blankness and momentary terror, as if the universe suddenly contained one less deity, but he didn't feel the kind of sadness he thought he would.

At the next corner he reached the town beach. A group of Italian men were playing bocci, and beyond them children were running after Frisbees in the sand. The economic level dropped as quickly in Bayside as it did in New York. The people at the beach lived in small one- or two-bedroom cottages with tiny lawns overflowing with azaleas or roses: the fiercely proud gardening of the lower middle class. The center of town consisted of only a few bars and restaurants, a general store and post office, and a casino where people danced as well as gambled.

It was a narrow but scrupulously clean beach that looked out at a new condominium complex (the Wainscott) across the bay, but he preferred its noisy chaos, its screaming babies and leaping dogs to the swimming pool society at the Ambassador.

It occurred to him that he'd never been to the beach with his father, but when he'd talked his mother into joining him, the two of them often had a good time. It was strange to remember such moments of pleasure between them. True, there were fewer of them the older he got, but he knew a secret world of such moments still lay just below the surface of everything else. One childhood memory was particularly strong. While she was correcting papers, he used to lie on her bed and call her by his favorite nicknames, until, feigning exasperation, she'd get up from her desk and join him on the bed. Then they'd laugh and kiss each other for what seemed like hours. This was one of his earliest memories, but he knew they'd done this until he was at least ten or eleven, the endless kissing running in a bizarre counterpoint to his terrible anger at her.

How had their fighting started? Who ultimately was at fault? It seemed to him he'd spent much of his life trying to figure out exactly where the blame lay. Thus he'd grown up half accusing his mother because she was his parent and should have known better, and half accusing himself because he was a child and was *ipso facto* wrong. Even now, in their latest dispute, he felt divided. She was wrong to taunt him about his career, to insult him again by calling his girlfriends "whores"; but at the same time he shouldn't have sworn at her or deserted her, especially now when she was so vulnerable. Besides, he was partially ashamed of his ulterior motives; he *had* wanted to get some money from her.

He walked past the bocci courts, then past the jungle gym and swings, until he reached the pier next to the casino. The pier extended about three hundred feet into the water. At its end fifteen or twenty men, some with their wives or grandsons, were fishing, while cranes and pelicans swirled about their heads or rested on the railing. It was a walk he had taken many times. Fifty feet from the end of the pier he saw a woman in a blue bathing suit. She had shining brown hair, blue eyes, and a long-limbed, graceful body.

As he watched her, pretending to observe the fishermen, he remembered with a kind of shame the almost insatiable lust he had felt from the time of his father's stroke until his death three months later. His casual girlfriend at the time was not enough for him, and he had sought out women at singles bars, and then prostitutes. He thought it was ridiculous to feel so much with strangers, but even sex with the prostitutes shook him to his bones. For a time he thought he'd crossed some magical threshold in his sex life, but shortly after his father's death it all returned to normal again.

He was trying to get the woman's attention but she continued sunbathing, apparently oblivious to him. Suddenly he saw an image of his mother's contorted mouth as she uttered the word "whore." He closed his eyes and replaced the image with a picture of her swimming up to him when he was a child, emerging from the water with a series of kisses for him. But this was immediately followed by a feeling of infinite regret and longing, and he gritted his teeth to fight against this guilt, this crippling tenderness that threatened him from all sides. Finally he was able to look toward the woman again, but she had left her spot—in fact, she was almost off the pier; if he didn't hurry he'd lose her.

She had a green blanket on the grass to the right of the swings and was already packing her things when he got to the beach. She appeared to hesitate for a moment, then, putting on her sunglasses, crossed the street and walked into a bar. Allen followed her at a discreet distance.

It was a plain bar, dark, with a small pool table and an understocked jukebox. When he first looked inside he didn't see her and a feeling of unreality swept through him. Then he saw her at a table next to the far window, eating a sandwich and sipping a soft drink. Normally he would have been frozen in such a situation, but as soon as he saw her he walked to the bar, ordered a beer, and took it to the table next to hers. She continued sipping her drink without looking at him.

"Excuse me," he said. "Weren't you out on the pier a few minutes ago?"

She turned her head a few degrees toward him, looking at him through her red-rimmed sunglasses, and said, "Could be."

"Are you here for a vacation?"

She hesitated. He grew afraid that he'd be answered with another "could be" or something equally laconic.

"You're from New York, aren't you?" she said with a trace of disdain.

"You've got a very good ear."

"I used to live there."

"Really? And where do you live now?"

"In a house, a nice little house."

"Here? In Bayside—or nearby?" Again there was a long pause, and he watched her taking birdlike nibbles of her sandwich.

"Nearby," she finally said. She removed her lipstick from her pocketbook and began redoing her lips.

"You work here? Or go to school?"

"Yeah, I work," she said vaguely. "Well, I've got to go now," she said, getting up suddenly. "Nice talking to you."

Before he could think of anything to say she was halfway to the door. He finished his beer and watched her cross the street. He was wondering how he could stop her before she got to her car, when she settled under a palm tree on the grassy part of the beach behind the jungle gym. Was this a sign for him to follow? She must have known he'd watch her from the window. He walked to the bar and paid for another bottle to take with him.

As soon as he turned the corner he looked for her again, half expecting not to see her. But she was in the same spot by the palm tree, her blue suit gleaming in the sun. He imagined himself approaching her, beer in hand, and decided that the beer might frighten her, so he finished it outside the bar as fast as he could. Then he stared at himself in the window by the bar and rearranged his hair. These last years he'd been fighting a constant battle with his hair as it continued to thin and recede. He finally assured himself that at least it wasn't gray yet and started walking toward the girl. He thought of how stubbornly his mother had fought to keep herself a convincing blonde, and then he closed his eyes to erase this new, unpleasant link between them. The girl was lying on her side looking through a movie magazine. He thought she must have seen him coming but he couldn't be sure, so he began speaking when he was still thirty feet away.

"So we meet again."

She didn't react immediately. It was as if she had not only seen him, but had also foreseen him. It occurred to him that she might be a prostitute.

"Oh, hello," she said tonelessly, and then turned back to her magazine. He was already angry that she'd left him so abruptly in the bar and had, in effect, lied to him. He was going to ask her about this but thought better of it.

"Do you mind if I sit down here?" he said with feigned casualness.

"Why should I mind?"

"What's the magazine you're reading?"

"*Silver Screen*," she answered, still without looking up. "It's a movie magazine."

"Are you an aspiring actress? I mean, would you like to be in the movies?"

"You're real curious about me, aren't you?"

"It's just that you've obviously got the looks to make it in the movies."

"Think so? My mother tells me I look a lot like Brooke Shields."

"You're prettier, actually."

"Maybe, but I'm definitely shorter."

"How old are you?"

"You taking a census or someting?"

"No, not at all," he said holding up his hands in protest. There was a minute of silence while he tried to think of another topic. The ease with which she returned to her magazine infuriated him, but coupled with this anger was a desire for her that continued to surprise him. At first he had been attracted to her general form, to the shape of her face and body. Now he noticed how clear and soft her skin was. He no longer wanted to know how old she was because he was afraid she was too young.

He decided to take advantage of her absorption in the magazine and quietly moved from his spot until he was sitting right beside her.

"Who are you reading about?"

"Drew Barrymore."

"Really? What's it say?"

"How she's changing her image. You know, from child star to a more, you know, mature image. And also how she's breaking away from her father, to like grow up more and not be so self-destructive."

"That's a hard thing to do."

"What?"

"To break away from your father, wouldn't you say?"

She looked at him quizzically, her mouth opening slightly, and finally shrugged her shoulders.

"Of course, I guess it's easier to do if you're as rich as she is."

The girl laughed, and he felt momentarily encouraged.

"What about you?" he said. "Are you close to your parents?"

She shrugged her shoulders again, and he noticed a pinched, slightly irritated expression returning to her eyes.

"I've really got to go soon," she said, looking at her wristwatch. The strap was the same color red as the rims of her sunglasses.

"You've got to go soon? But you just got here."

"Yeah, and now I'm going to go."

"I hope I wasn't bothering you." He was forcing himself not to look at her face, but he couldn't keep from staring at her legs.

"Why would I let you bother me?"

"I guess I'm just disappointed that you're leaving. I really like talking to you."

"Yeah, well, someone's waiting for me."

"Could I call you?"

"I don't think so. I'm going with someone."

"Oh. Of course."

He said this in what he hoped was a convincing tone of acceptance, but he was angry. Moreover, he felt a sudden impulse to touch her, perhaps to kiss her, but certainly to touch her.

He began making jokes, improvised remarks about the old people on the beach, the dogs running around in circles, somehow a link from that to the movies, to Brooke Shields and Drew Barrymore. His last remark won a smile from her, and his hand fell on her leg just above her knee.

"What are you doing?" she said in a voice whose tone suddenly went hollow.

"You're so pretty when you smile. I'm just telling you you have an incredible smile, that's all."

"Will you take your hand off me?"

"Sure," he said. But he didn't.

"It won't go," he said, hoping to make her laugh again. He now actually had both his hands on her upper thighs. The girl made an effort to get up, but he increased the pressure.

"Listen, asshole, take your hands off or I'll scream for help. I'll get the cops over here. Don't you know there are cops all over this beach?"

"Don't get excited," he said. He intended to cooperate now, but before he could move she dug her nails into his hands and hissed at him, "Get off me, you freak!" Her lower teeth were jutting out as she stood up and he began to back away from her slowly and unsteadily, inadvertently holding his hands up as if she were pointing a gun at him. She tried to snatch up her blanket without bending over, and the magazine fell off it. Instinctively he went to pick it up but she said, "Don't touch that. Don't you ever touch a thing of mine."

"I'm sorry, I'm really sorry," he said, backing away from her slowly. "I'm going now."

"You come down to an old people's beach just to scare women. You're sick."

A few of the old couples had now turned to stare at him with the placid bewilderment of fish that had suddenly been disturbed. He began to walk briskly toward the casino, her final shriek of "maniac" filling the air behind him.

He was very worried now. Had the lifeguard been on duty? If so, could he hear her from his chair? And what about the police? She was nearly hysterical, as much from anger as from fear. Would she call them?

He decided to take a back road behind the casino that would lead in a more roundabout way to the Ambassador. He thought it would be best to walk calmly, but soon he found himself breaking into a run. If stopped, he'd pretend he was jogging.

Over and over he repeated the scene with the girl, reassuring himself that he hadn't really done anything. What was the matter with him, he thought, looking over his shoulders as he ran. Why was he acting like such an incompetent child? He must have thought the girl was leading him on. He must have misunderstood her.

When he reached the tennis court he stopped running. The old man was still playing, clinging to his racket as if it were a lifesaver, while his grandson stayed crouched on the baseline, waiting to pounce on his serve. Again Allen looked over his shoulder but no one was behind him. Finally he began to wipe away the perspiration streaming down his face as if it too was out of control.

Should he take a shower by the pool before going home? He decided not to. People would stare at him and whisper. Someone would perhaps connect him to his mother and say something to her later. One of them might even sense what he had done. In spite of their collective stupor, one of them might spontaneously rise up from his chaise longue and pronounce him guilty.

He passed by the parking lots and shuffleboard courts. The sky had turned as white as the condominiums. His heart was pounding rapidly as he ran up the stairs instead of taking the elevator.

At the door he wiped his face with both sleeves, still looking behind himself. Everything was white and still, the people by the pool like figures in a painting. He let himself in with his key, fully expecting to see his mother standing in front of him, but the hallway and living room billowed in front of him like a continuation of the silent tableau he'd left outside. He thought something terrible might have happened to his mother. Just before he opened her door he imagined she might have swallowed too many sleeping pills.

He opened her bedroom door without knocking and she gave a little cry from her chair in front of the dressing table.

"You startled me!" she said, more embarrassed than angry. He quickly said he was sorry. She had combed her hair out, wet and thin and grayer than he had ever seen it, and was furiously applying hair coloring to it.

"This is what I have to do to make myself presentable in this world."

"You don't need to," he said softly. She suddenly recalled her wound and turned her eyes from him bitterly.

"You told me you'd rather be dead than live with me. Nice. Very nice."

"I didn't mean it."

He wanted to apologize deeply, immediately, to proclaim his love for her and embrace her, but before he could she began describing the dangers of peroxide.

"I'm probably combing cancer into my hair every time I do this, but I do it to stay pretty."

"You're always pretty," he said in his most earnest voice, the voice he had used to speak to her twenty years before.

"You're a liar, but thank you."

"Listen, I took a walk and thought things over. I'm really sorry for everything."

She smiled slightly but turned away from him when he tried to give her a hug. He fought down his anger, hoping to keep alive the spark of love he was feeling.

"Well, I'm glad you've come to your senses," she said, pulling herself up to her full height in the chair and assuming her most mature tone of voice. "I don't know why you like to hurt me so much. I guess I've spoiled you, so it's my fault and I should accept the blame." She sighed deeply. "Now, Allen darling, wait in the living room for ten minutes until this cancer junk dries and then, if you still want to, maybe you can give your old mother a kiss."

Heidi Indoors

It's raining this morning. People will be upset. The mail could be delayed for—it's impossible to say precisely how long the mail will be delayed. But it so seldom rains in Santa Vista that it will surely be viewed as a calamity, especially since it's raining hard. When the natives speak of rain they usually mean something so discreet it barely makes an impression on the air. Here is a central paradox of Santa Vista: trees and flowers abound of inconceivable richness and variety, the city fairly sparkles, and yet it rarely rains. How is this possible? The answer is simply that Santa Vistans have become experts in water management. The entire hierarchy, from the local government to the most humble homeowner, is constantly thinking about and using water in ingenious ways. Moreover, people are perpetually washing, cleaning, and scrubbing with such proficiency that Santa Vista is now as white as it is blue and green and golden.

When one cleans so devotedly, one soon cultivates an acute sense of order as well. An argument I overheard between two ten-year-old boys in the town's largest park no longer seems strange to me. One had accused the other of removing a rock from the side of a brook. He didn't accuse the boy of stealing it, simply rearranging it, for his sense of design was already sophisticated enough to feel violated by any variation in the park.

Yet in this passion for cleanliness and order lies another paradox, for it sometimes leads to needless repetition and ultimately to insidious disorders. Case in point: It was felt the transit center needed repaving, although in my estimation, admittedly influenced by experiencing so many potholes in New York, the cement was already impressively smooth. As a result, the sites for all local buses, as well as those destined for Los Angeles and beyond, had to be moved. For weeks people were no longer certain where to find the buses or when they were leaving. Everything returned to normal only when the center reopened, apparently with a fresh layer of cement, and with the round transit building, which houses the ticket office, gleaming under yet another coat of superfluous white paint.

With dreamlike suddenness the rain stops and the sky rearranges itself quickly into its characteristic blue. I knock on Heidi's door twice to signal the end of the rain and she returns one knock, which means she doesn't want to take a walk with me. I'm living with Heidi, although I make frequent use of my adjoining apartment. It's very easy to "live with" someone in Santa Vista, but at first I didn't understand. Last year, when I arrived from New York to teach French literature at the University of Isla Vista, I spent a year of extreme, almost intolerable, isolation. My only companions were books, which I admit I love to a fault.

Maybe in some ways I courted my situation. Before deciding to leave New York, I'd just finished *Remembrance of Things Past*, reading it, I'm afraid, more for its therapeutic value than for its literary charms. I saw myself all too easily as Swann and then Marcel and the women in my past, particularly the one who'd just left me, as either Odette or Albertine. It was as much to escape my own Albertine as for the not particularly prestigious position in Santa Vista that I left my university behind in New York.

In the very beginning I was encouraged. I thought Santa Vista with its consistently soothing weather would be an ideal place for me to adopt a more sunny, stable disposition. Certainly the climate had none of the hysteria of New York (or France). I went to the nearby beach eagerly, but as soon as I spotted an attractive sunbather I'd stop myself. I was afraid of my own impulses, and even more afraid I was no longer entertaining enough to hold a woman's interest for even a few minutes. In that sense Heidi helped me a great deal, though I could hardly imagine the way she'd accomplish this, nor what the consequences would be.

Despite Heidi's refusal I decide to take a walk while there are still some clouds out, admittedly already racing away. You must understand that to see a solid cloud here, even one already in the process of disappearing, is a rare thing.

In Santa Vista it's also possible to walk for several blocks without seeing anyone else walking. But people are moving by you all the time in cars, on bicycles, on skateboards, or else simply running by. Walking down Anapamu Street I notice the startled eyes of an old man moving awkwardly to just avoid a fleet of oncoming boys on racing bikes. It's more reassuring perhaps to look at the ocean under the now-full sun. I can even see, looking like they're only several yards apart, the long, even row of oil rigs. Oil is being sought all along the coast. At night they light the boats up to resemble Christmas trees and most people consider it a romantic sight. Many couples have decided to live together while watching those lights.

On the way to the center of town I pass cross streets named Carrillo, Canon Perdido, De La Guerra, Cervantes. The Spanish or Mexican influence is as strong in Santa Vista as in the rest of California, perhaps stronger. One sees it not only in the street names, of course, but in the restaurants and architecture. There is even supposed to be a large population of Mexicans, but one sees them about as often as one sights a cloud. They live in the closest thing to a slum in Santa Vista, at the bottom of State Street. State Street, however, in its grandest spots is a line of radiant restaurants and elegant shops—with the mountains of Montecito as a backdrop, and the harbor and Channel Islands visible from any point. It is, shall we say, the Fifth Avenue of Santa Vista. In fact, as one walks by its palm trees and fountains, one understands, if only for a moment, why Santa Vistans often refer to their town as Paradise.

I select a rather unlikely place in Paradise to have my lunch. I decide to eat at the Copper Coffee Pot, a cafeteria that caters to old people. I think I go there because of my memory of the old man dodging the bicycle. He'd probably strayed from one of the senior citizens homes in the foothills. There was something in his expression—a desire not to intrude on the cyclists' need for exercise even as he tried, politely, to save his life—that was very poignant.

It was while I was bent over my (of all things!) New England boiled dinner that I suddenly recalled the chain of circumstances that led me to my present situation with Heidi. It began during one of my walks when I spotted a sign (in the window of the Copper Coffee Pot, actually) announcing the Annual Writers of Santa Vista Reading in The Good Earth Bookstore. I interpreted this as a true sign of Providence, for here would be my best chance yet to meet someone.

I almost said to myself "anyone," for I was emotionally ravenous. My days then centered around the delivery of the mail or my staring sessions at the telephone, as if I believed I could somehow will it into ringing. My nights were devoted to semi-successful attempts to sleep. As for my work at the university, the people there were too homogenous, too relentlessly polite. My students were essentially indistinguishable: a bland blonde block of overdomesticated teenagers. It was not only with excitement that I went to the reading, but in my quasi-hysterical melancholy I already thought of it as my last chance.

The reading was long (The Good Earth naturally didn't want to offend any Santa Vistans who considered themselves writers) and filled with old people, though quite a few children wandered in with their well-scrubbed pets and simply sat down on the floor. Food and drink and laughter and unabashed tributes filled the air. Sweet readings of this nature can hardly be conceived of in New York.

There was one reader named Estar who especially intrigued me. It was not because I was attracted to her—she was about twenty years older than me—but because her prose was more lucid than the others and her personality seemed accessible as well. When I called her the next day and introduced myself as an admirer of her work, she seemed very eager for me to visit and went over the directions to her house several times.

Estar lived on the mesa in a house directly overlooking the ocean and the Channel Islands. Like all the women in her circle, she was wealthy, separated from her spouse, and lived days that were full of leisure. In fact, this circle descended on us shortly after I arrived and I spent only fifteen minutes alone with her.

"I don't do much one-to-one talking," she informed me from the chaise longue on her terrace, where she was smoking marijuana from a large water pipe. "I keep myself amused by being around groups of interesting people."

She offered me some of her homegrown sensimelli; I politely declined and settled on a beer. Her skin had a vital tightness that contrasted dramatically with the increasingly vacant look in her eyes.

"How do you find Santa Vista? But that's like asking how do you find paradise, 'cause it really is paradise here. Believe me," she continued, "I've lived everywhere in the world and this is the best."

The "interesting people" arrived then and soon joined us on the terrace. Each of the women was between forty and fifty-five, was heavily made up, and could barely fit into her jeans. Yet I hesitate to make fun of Estar's little clan, for a few minutes later Heidi arrived. She had long blonde hair—nothing unusual about that; most people in Santa Vista are blonde—but Heidi's wasn't bleached—for she was still somewhere in her thirties. I also noticed that she fit into her jeans much more easily than her colleagues; in fact, she fit into them quite nicely. I tried not to stare at her too obviously as she easily joined the conversation, which ranged from the quality of their homegrown pot, to their therapists (most were "holistic" that year), to their ex-husbands, then back to the pot again. Someone told Estar that if she kept chain-smoking marijuana she'd eventually get cancer. The group (including Estar) laughed—but Heidi screamed. My remarks about order notwithstanding, screams occur frequently in Santa Vista; however, they usually happen in the context of Holistic Inner Space Channeling or some other therapeutic setting and virtually never on a back porch.

Heidi herself seemed most surprised of all. She stood up and two full tears jumped like skiers from a slope, one from each eye. She received bear hugs from everyone (everyone but a shy and fascinated me), but there was no consoling her. The scream had been too shrill, too intense. A few minutes later she left.

Now, of course, there was something new to talk about. To bring me up to date Estar explained that Heidi had just had a completely successful operation for skin cancer a few weeks ago. Apparently she was more "into the experience" than anyone realized. Sometime before the afternoon ended I was urged to visit her. I then discovered the amazing fact that she lived in my apartment complex (having only recently been separated, she'd moved in about a month before I did), and only two doors away.

I emphasize again, there is very little left here of New England Puritanism. It's as if that's all been absorbed by the sun. It seemed strangely natural that at the end of my visit (after we took one of our last walks together) I went to bed with Heidi. While we talked I was quite sympathetic, and sincerely so. But any reference, however arcane, to her scream embarrassed her and she quickly steered the conversation toward her divorce and her husband's numerous deficiencies.

How does it happen that people become devoted to one another so quickly, at least enough to decide to live together, if only for a while? Within a week we spent each night together, but already problems were developing. Already she was very reluctant to go outside.

It's been almost a week since Heidi's been outdoors. We have not discussed at any length, or in any detail, why she stays in her apartment.

For a few days she tried to hide it. She'd make excuses (mostly involving her husband, Harold, who she said was spying on her) about why she didn't want to go to the beach or to a restaurant or even shopping. When I'd press her about this she'd pick a fight and I'd immediately back down.

I am being very careful. I am walking on eggshells about this. You must understand that even if I asked her directly I wouldn't necessarily get a complete answer. Heidi is what therapists are fond of calling an indirect communicator. She communicates through analogy or omission more than through immediate response. It's from such oblique signs that I've pieced together the reasons for her sudden aversion to the outdoors.

Her main fear, incongruous as it might be in Santa Vista, is of contamination. Although I was assured that her cure was completely successful, she fears that something in the street or air, some germ, will bring back her cancer. I am not sure this is the only reason, but her anger when I've questioned her about this has been so strong that I've stopped asking.

As for her friends, they have been told stories, or she has told the same story various ways. Taking advantage of the high esteem in which all forms of spiritual self-exercise are held, she told them that she is "in retreat" and will contact them when it is over. So great is her credibility, or so gullible are her friends, that the phone hasn't rung for days. No one has questioned or apparently doubted her, and I remain her only link to what's outside.

But what of our life together in her apartment? I am still permitted to go outside, though I try to restrict the number of times I leave her alone. Let's say I return from a brief trip to school. I am greeted by a rapid fluttering of eyelids. She doesn't specifically request it, but she stares so mournfully in that direction that I take a shower, staying in perhaps five minutes longer than I normally would, the better to convince her that I'm completely disinfected.

I am not asked what I did or where I've been. Instead, I'm treated with a kind of cool hostility, as if by being outside I've betrayed her. This hostility is short lived. There is so much for her to do—in fact, the next time I look at her she's already by the window pretending to dust an area so clean it's already blinding, but actually checking for cracks, slits, openings, any place where air from outside could find a way in.

To get back on her good side, I pretend to review her "window checking" without precisely mimicking her gestures—which might have the effect of insulting her. In the same spirit I also assist with her cleaning (the entire apartment is systematically cleaned three times a day), often adopting the least glamorous places to clean, like the bathroom.

Still, it would be a big mistake to think that because Heidi has given up certain formerly prominent activities in her life (like swimming, surfing, bicycling—indeed, the entire outdoors) her personality has also undergone a metamorphosis. She's lost neither her sense of humor, her powers of organization, nor her sensuality—all have simply been transferred or readjusted to a world sealed off from the outside. It would also be incorrect to assume that our whole day is spent working and worrying. We even have regular "playtime" incorporated into our schedule.

During playtime we often have sex, which Heidi always keeps varied and exciting, and we often read and listen to music, although certain records (like Debussy's "La Mer") are considered in poor taste and are never played. Even nonprogramatic classical music makes Heidi melancholy, so I've learned not to play it. To help cheer me up Heidi started turning on a soft rock station on the radio and we've begun dancing. We've also begun to take great pleasure in our meals, which have been reduced to two a day as our food supply continues to diminish. Heidi, whose diet reflects the characteristic Santa Vistan preoccupation with physical fitness, fairly caresses her figs and granola, her assorted grains and cooked seaweed before she digests them. It's no different with me, although my food, which I brought from my apartment, reflects my Manhattan origins and consists primarily of Triscuits, canned tuna fish, Cheerios, and Rice-A-Roni. Just as our sensitivity to taste has increased, so has our sense of sight. Although there are now fewer things to look at, we cherish them more than when we had all of the outdoors to look at. In the white drapes, for instance, which are always closed, I now find a subtle and shifting beauty, whose tints and textures are constantly altered by the angle of the sun. Sometimes when Heidi is in the kitchen cleaning, I can't resist parting them a few inches, as if I were parting a woman's lips, to get a glimpse of the inevitable blue sky or the green palm trees outside.

I'll tell you what else. Her imagination has not atrophied either. For example: We began to realize that we were watching too much TV. As an alternative, Heidi began to invent games. There was "Hospital," which revolved around trying to save a patient on a life-support system from a maniacal killer; "Museum," which concerned a hunt for an inauthentic "masterpiece" that would cost the museum millions of dollars if not found among the three floors of art; and her most autobiographical creation, "Divorce Spy," which featured blockades and safety spaces and was played a little like Parcheesi.

Finally, I want to emphasize that, for the most part, her empathy, her generosity of spirit remained constant. Once after a game of "Divorce Spy" I mentioned that I'd run out of sleeping pills and needed to see my therapist in town to renew my prescription.

"You don't need to see your doctor. I promise you you can get to sleep without him," Heidi said.

"How can I, without the pills?"

"I'm sure I can get you to sleep," she said, winking at me meaningfully.

That night I was the lucky recipient of her most indefatigable seduction to date. I went to sleep—after a few hours—dreaming of a bar of sunlight.

My point is that a relationship can survive (at least for a time) without going outside. Human beings are nothing if not masters of adaptation. Moreover, we must always have known this about ourselves. How else could the Fallout Shelterists of the '50s and their heirs, the Survivalists of the '80s, envision life? They too were fighting a war with the outside, or at the very least planning to cut themselves off from it. I've also heard of people in Las Vegas who choose always to live inside. Isn't the essence of that city indoors anyway?

So, yes, I decided to join Heidi in her curious vigil (it was between terms and I wasn't yet jeopardizing my job), but I reassured myself that it would by no means be a permanent commitment. I'm doing it with the hope that if I stay inside with her and submit to all her rituals and requirements, she may slowly trust me enough to join me outside in a walk to the store, where soon I'll have to buy food anyway, not to mention those household goods necessary for maintaining her high standards of sanitation.

Meanwhile, certain tensions in our relationship have eased. For instance, the constant references to her husband, Harold, have diminished. These were especially nettlesome when they occurred, as they invariably did, around and about our time in bed. If she didn't actually invoke him before sex, as if to ward off what she was about to do, it occurred afterward and had the effect of undermining what had just happened. Moreover, it struck me as unfair that she could allude to countless scenes of backpacking and surfing with Harold, whereas I wasn't even allowed to play "La Mer" much less mention the outdoors. When she realized that she'd hurt me, she'd quickly deny that he had any deep appeal for her. They had simply spent so much time with each other, in effect growing up together in Santa Vista, that he was all she knew. Maybe, she conceded, he had tried so hard to possess her that she still felt "married" to him, although she certainly "loathed" him now.

At any rate, her references to Harold began to stop. I'm convinced my staying inside with her was directly related to this. Once at the end of cleaning she said: "You know, Harold would never do this for me."

"You mean clean the house?"

"No, no, darling. What you're doing by staying here with me."

I smiled and let the matter drop. In many ways I was quite in love. For example, I was fascinated with virtually every part of her body (her golden hair, her firm rear end, her minute toes) and was happily content to view it exclusively, instead of the geography of the Earth, at least for a while. If she considered what I was doing a sacrifice, that was both touching and all to the good. That she rewarded me by speaking less of her husband and her impending divorce was an extra, undreamed of benefit.

Was it two weeks, or three? Could two people stay in a one-bedroom apartment in Santa Vista that long while the sun was so bright it poured through the window, although the blinds were drawn hermetically tight? Apparently it happened and happened quite happily; each day, of course, having a certain déjà vu quality about it. There were always our meals, a few hours of playtime, and our constant cleaning, which she finally assured me wasn't motivated by her fear of cancer.

"Is that why you think I'm staying in?" she said, looking up with an astonished smile from her sponge and Lysol.

"I don't know."

"People don't get cancer from the sun alone, though I'm fair-skinned, and, of course, too much sun would be dangerous."

"Why are you staying in then?"

"Because of Harold. I thought I told you that. He's hired a man to spy on me just to rattle me before the trial. I want to frustrate him for a while, that's all. Let him sit outside and learn nothing."

I was skeptical but returned to my coursework.

That evening in bed Heidi put down *The Fate of the Earth*, in which she'd been deeply absorbed, and said, "Did you know that a nuclear bomb is just like letting the Sun meet the Earth?"

"I think I've figured it out," Heidi said.

"What's that?" I asked. We were lying in bed, propped up by four pillows, watching the late news.

"Why you don't believe I have to stay inside."

"I believe you."

"But you don't really understand."

"Understanding and believing aren't the same, are they?"

"It's because you're a real left brain person and I'm right brain. But most people in New York are left brain, aren't they? I mean, you have to be real rational to live there, don't you?"

"I assure you New York is full of irrational people."

"But it must be real different there. I mean, it's so big and fast moving, nobody could follow you there. Nobody could really spy on you."

"It would be different, but they could do it; it's done all the time."

"Or take the sun, it's blocked out by the buildings, isn't it? I wouldn't have got skin cancer there."

"You might have or you might not have. But in general it's much safer here than in New York, you can be sure of that."

Heidi nodded, but not very convincingly, then got up suddenly and turned down the TV.

"Did you hear that noise outside?"

"No."

"Listen."

"It's nothing, it's the wind."

"The wind isn't nothing."

"I meant it's not a person outside."

"Think so?"

It occurred to me more than once that Heidi was using her "reasons" for staying inside as a smokescreen to hide a deeper fear. Of course, I realized she was probably unaware of her own motivations, as people often are. It all reminded me of the way certain people just can't be happy on their vacation and will complain constantly about almost imperceptible inconveniences simply because, for one reason or another, they aren't "ready" to vacation. They're guilty or they're angry at themselves. In short, they're unprepared for the consequences of pleasure.

You can see I was giving Heidi's situation a good deal of thought, and in that sense I was living a kind of double life in those days. On the one hand I was the same overeager lover, the same confidant for her latest suspicions about her husband, or "the unhealthy and positively dangerous levels of radiation that already exist." But secretly I was trying to understand why we were living this way, even though (or perhaps because) I was also so strangely gratified.

Finally, a change. I had to go out to buy food. We'd been

eating out of cans and packages for almost a week. Besides, if I wanted to keep my job I had to go to work the next day anyway. I'd already canceled two days' worth of classes. As if sensing all this, Heidi began a remarkably inventive lovemaking game (part of it involving the last scraps of food in the refrigerator) so that we were lying naked beside each other when I spoke.

"There's no food left. I'll have to do some shopping."

She rolled over on her side, her back turned to the window where the curtains and shades behind them had been drawn for weeks. I thought I saw a tremor pass through her lovely shoulders.

"You mean right now? You know, of course, that Harold probably has a man right outside the house."

"I'll be back in ten, in five minutes."

She got out of bed and began slipping on her bra and panties in the magically quick and quiet way women can do this.

"Look, stay by the phone and if there's any trouble call the police."

A long silence followed, which I decided to interpret as a form of acceptance or resignation. Immediately I dressed and left her apartment.

Outside it was more ravishing than I'd imagined or feared. The sky was aqua, the ocean lapis lazuli and blazing white from the sunshine. I was struck by the enormous size and thickness of the magnolia trees, the fig trees, the sycamores, and, of course, the palms. The ice plant was turning red in spots, sign of a subtle Santa Vista winter, and the air seemed to be full of the scent of flowers. People were smiling as they ran or cycled by. The Oriental woman behind the counter in the 7-Eleven looked like an angel. This really is paradise, I said to myself softly.

When I returned, I communicated none of my impressions to Heidi. Instead I acted as if I'd fulfilled a painful but necessary duty and made a point of setting down each item I bought on the counter and announcing it loudly to reemphasize why I'd gone outside. I found myself saying "Jack cheese, skim milk,

Lysol," etc., to the empty kitchen, for Heidi was staying in her bedroom.

Apparently she'd decided to punish me through a demonstrable lack of enthusiasm for me and my doings. She was almost completely withdrawn during dinner and, after deciding against both dancing or playing any of the games, she'd quickly retreated to her room again. When I eventually followed, I found her in her closet.

"What are you doing? Are you cleaning?"

"I'm rearranging," she said, as she began taking her wedding and honeymoon pictures out of her closet, displaying them on her bureau and bedroom desk. She was particularly fond of a photograph of Harold and her surfing, each with an arm linked around the other's waist, during a trip they took to Carpinteria. I pretended not to notice. I simply closed my eyes and let my memories of the outdoors dazzle me until I slept.

The next morning I decided not to talk about going to the university. I did, however, leave a detailed note explaining where and why I was going and exactly when I'd be back.

I could hardly lecture (though God knows I'd had a good deal of time to prepare) I was so overwhelmed by so much sudden human company. My students, whom I'd previously considered so depressingly homogenous, seemed infinitely varied and resonant. Time flew by and I found myself astonished by the subtleties of their behavior. In the state I was in, I decided to leave work before I got into any long conversations.

By the time I started my walk back to Heidi's, it was already past sunset. At night Santa Vista all but closes down. Only on Saturday night can you see even a few couples strolling down State Street. I already could see people scurrying into restaurants or toward their cars as if a storm were coming, instead of simply darkness. However, there were still beautiful things to see. There was the intense rose light of the Granada Movie Theater marquee, the lighted clock on top of the courthouse, the whole meticulously manicured courthouse lawn bathed in a lemon-colored light. There was the umbrella formed by the evergreens on Olive Street, and the town high school, illuminated by a golden light, recessed far off Cervantes Street, large and clean and spectacularly deserted like a Moorish castle.

I was so transported by the richness I saw everywhere that I was determined to share my revelations with Heidi. I knocked on her door vigorously, but got no answer. I knocked again, making sure I was doing it in the sequence we'd devised to "communicate safely." Only as a last resort did I approach her window, calling out her name and then my own. Finally I walked over two doors to the right and called her from my own apartment. Again no answer. Just as I was about to call the police (for I was now really worried) she answered one of my calls.

"Heidi, why didn't you answer me? What's happened?"

"I have nothing to say to you anymore."

"I don't understand."

"You made your choice, now I've made mine."

"Choice? I had no choice. I had to go to work."

"You left me in a state of great danger. I'd say you had a choice."

"Heidi, your fears are ridiculous, unfounded. There's nothing outside that's dangerous—it's merely in your mind that—"

"You, however, are no longer in my mind. Please don't call again."

Then she hung up. Feeling defeated, at least for the night, I promptly began drinking myself to sleep.

Of course in the next days I made many more calls which were unanswered or which she disconnected as soon as I spoke. I also slipped letters, entreaties, apologies under her door, none of which she replied to. After two weeks I stopped trying. I continued my teaching, my walks. I even half-heartedly visited a few singles bars, with no particular results. Need I add that my fleeting vision of Santa Vista as a paradise deserted me as well, never to return.

It's raining again. Little specks of rain like the finest motes of dust fall out of the sky, look discouraged halfway down, and evaporate before they reach the ground. This morning I prefer it this way—Santa Vista under a rare gray sky. It's spring break and I'm leaving for New York. I have a few job possibilities at other schools, nothing definite, but some worth exploring. In fact, even if nothing definite materializes I've decided to move East in June and live on unemployment if necessary. I've already told my chairman at the university. He smiled and was naturally polite about it.

I haven't seen Heidi in more than three months. After I stopped my barrage of phone calls and letters I did from time to time linger outside her bedroom window where the blinds remained shut, the shades drawn, hoping for some kind of sign, perhaps a trace of her cleaning, but these watches never produced a result.

I also made a few inquiries that got me nowhere. Discretion, like silence, is practiced religiously in Santa Vista. As long as you pay your rent and are quiet, no building manager will ever betray you.

While I'm waiting for a taxi to the airport the rain stops. The sun covers everything again, as if it had never left; indeed, one can't even see a sign of a rainbow.

When the cab arrives we begin to travel down Anapamu Street. All the residents of Paradise seem to be out on the streets celebrating. The air is filled with flying Frisbees, skateboards, bicycles and wide, blue-eyed smiles. At a stoplight I notice a curious couple. They are moving so slowly and furtively that from the back I thought they were from a senior citizens home, but as they pass us at our long red light I see that they're my age. The woman is so bundled up with scarves that hardly any of her face is visible. Still, of course, I recognize her at once, if only by a loop of golden hair. I'm about to tell the driver to stop when I notice that the man who seems to be guiding her, and at any rate is holding her hand very tightly, is someone I've seen before in photographs. It is none other than Harold, so I politely urge the driver to move on.

Vivian and Sid

You'd think that after fifty years people are as set in their ways as stones. Sophocles thought so, Faulkner thought so, but it isn't always the case. Just a few months ago I woke up one morning thinking there are too many TV channels, too many books getting published, and too many memories ready to pounce on me if I allow it. I had recently drifted into menopause, not really realizing it until I suffered one of those notorious hot flashes during my lecture on *Don Quixote*. Soon I started perspiring so much it was like I was doing construction work in the desert. So no, I was not feeling attractive or sexy or even very much like a woman. On the other hand, I'm something of an incurable optimist whose whole life's philosophy has been turning negatives into positives. Case in point: At the university where I began eighteen years ago as a non-tenure-track visiting lecturer I've survived five different chairmen, four different deans, and a variety of devious colleagues to become a full professor of comparative literature. A second case in point: I took a man, Sid, who thought he hated women, who screamed at me that he hated me in particular thirteen years ago in couples therapy, and we've stayed together all these years and built a life of relative peace and dignity. (Despite his nearly hysterical fears, he got his tenure, too, in the sociology department, although he remains an associate professor.)

In many ways Sid and I have had a remarkably open life. I think we never bothered to get married because there was so much communication so quickly; marriage seemed almost su-

perfluous. Often it felt like we'd discussed everything. Our decision not to have children and the related one not to marry
were analyzed year after year from every vantage point. It was
a mutual decision—we were both so ambitious and needy, it
didn't seem wise. We foresaw that there'd be some pain in being
childless, but it allowed us to spend lots of time together, which
we both realized we needed. I looked at Sid, sleeping fairly
contentedly that morning, and thought that if he suddenly found
out I literally was no longer a woman it probably wouldn't
change a thing.

The problem wasn't Sid, it was that I felt stalked down and
raped first by nature, and then by these horribly painful memories of when I was young and menstruating like a river and
having sex a lot and fantasizing about having children. It was
in the increasingly disturbing quiet of my Brookline apartment
that morning that I started to envision a way out. I called it
Project Memory Control. At the time it meant nothing less than
the radical reduction and restructuring of my entire memory.
But a grandiose statement like that requires some additional
explanation.

In my first fifty years of life I've probably had about the same
number of involuntary memories (as Proust called them) as the
next person. Sid would say more, since he's often accused me
of being a closet sentimentalist who idealizes her past. At such
times I'd invariably respond that sentimentality is just a form
of self-flattery and that I'm very clear about my past. This is
an example of the absurd and trifling arguments we've had
intermittently throughout our long relationship. What is certain
is that I was never afraid of my memories, and I never tried to
control them any more than I ever tried to regulate my periods.
Let them both bleed, was my unspoken motto. But after my
change, just when I was no longer physiologically capable of
being pregnant, I suddenly found my mind full of searing
memories.

I looked to literature, as I often do, for help. One of the
characters I found myself most identifying with, despite our
different genders, was Jake in *The Sun Also Rises.* He was

rendered impotent from a war wound and so was unable to consummate his love for Brett. Jake survived because of a tough inner discipline—true, there were all his routines and rituals—his work, his swimming and drinking and the bullfights he attended, but the key was his capacity to internally adjust his mental approach to reality. Couldn't I do something similar with my memory?

The answer proved to be, I absolutely could. I turned to television, of all things, for my next model. Sid made us subscribe to all the cable channels in Boston. Ever since the onset of his tenure case he'd used TV as both a tranquilizer and a source of escape. That he'd now had tenure for two and a half years and continued to watch an embarrassing amount of TV was something we also occasionally had words about.

I would watch him pressing his remote control from the recliner in our living room, "touring" as he called it through a dizzying galaxy of channels. I was staggered by their number and redundancy. For example, there were now two cable channels devoted exclusively to comedy. One was called, wittily enough, "The Comedy Channel"; the other was more pithily titled "Ha." Clearly the best offerings of these two absurdly padded channels could be merged without any loss to the viewer. And just as clearly there was no need for more than eight channels instead of the eighty-six we had access to; in fact, four would be more like it. But rather than putting my efforts into streamlining television channels, might I not apply the same principle to my memories?

Convert, Merge, Streamline became the watchwords of Project Memory Control. After a week or so of intermittent but intense meditation (I canceled office hours, deferred a couple of classes, and stayed away from Sid as much as possible) I'd reduced my memories to sixteen basic units or channels. Here's how it worked. Let's say I began to have a memory about one of the relatively few lovers I had before Sid. I'd classify this as "Another Man Memory." At the moment of impact I would "turn on" memory channel SAM, named for Beckett, whose story "The Expelled" ends with this truism: "Living souls you

will see how alike they are." Since the meaning of the line is
that we're all essentially the same person, it acted as an effective
filter to convert the potential new memory of another man into
one of my happiest memories with Sid, when we were kissing
for hours in the sand dunes of Provincetown the first summer
after he moved in.

I'll give two more examples. I haven't always had big thighs,
a big stomach, and a quasi-endless rear end. I used to look a
lot better, and lately I'd been prone to visual images of my
younger self. At those moments I began to press channel P for
Proust and to focus on the scene in *Remembrance of Things
Past* where Marcel meets his former childhood obsession, Gil-
berte, at a party thirty years later; he barely recognizes her and
can scarcely force himself to pay attention to the dowdy, disappointing woman she has become. The whole ending of Proust's
Swann's Way is also excellent on this subject. Using channel P
as a filter, I focused on a picnic Sid and I took at Walden Pond
ten years ago. I was already spreading out a bit then, as they
say, but it was a sunny day, which lit up my blue eyes I suppose.
I wore a pretty dress, Sid was in a happy mood and, in short,
he swears it was the best I ever looked. He claims that day he
fell in love with my soul, which he also swears was revealed
en toto on my face. (You see, he can be a sentimentalist, too.)

Now for the last example. When I was in graduate school I
was very ambitious; I wanted to be a female Northrop Frye.
Later, when I started teaching, I wanted to be more of a practical
critic and essayist, an Edmund Wilson or a George Steiner. (Sid,
whom I met at that time, wanted to be a Herbert Marcuse or
Norman O. Brown.) I published my dissertation on Proust and
Machado de Assis' *Epitaph of a Small Winner.* I've since published several articles in scholarly journals, done some transla-
tions and book reviews, but that's been about it. Recently, lines
from my more ambitious but abandoned projects had been floating through my mind, a most dangerous and insidious kind of
memory. Armed with memory control I would press channel
TB (for Thomas Bernhard, an Austrian writer Sid introduced
me to, correctly guessing how much I'd admire him) and I'd

recall these lines from Bernhard's brilliant novel *Concrete:* "We publish only to satisfy our craving for fame; there's no other motive except the even baser one of making money. . . . To publish anything is folly and evidence of a certain defect of character. To publish the intellect is the most heinous of all crimes." I remember how hard Sid and I laughed when he read me those lines in bed, and then how tightly we hugged each other afterward.

The thirteen other channels, each with their literary filters ranging from Shakespeare and Singer to Donne and Dylan Thomas, all worked in a similar way. My success ratio wasn't a hundred percent, but it was well above fifty, and as it approached seventy-five I began to feel appreciably better, as if life were giving me a present every day. (A lot of my physical symptoms seemed to improve too, including my dizziness and backaches; but I'll spare you those details.) I even began to get conceited in a way. I'm finally putting my literary training to a truly original use, I would often say to myself. Memory Control has become my art form.

But I'd kept all this a secret for too long. It was spring break, and classes were over for both of us. I knew it was time to tell Sid.

"What are you talking about Memory Control? What kind of meshugga B.S. is this?" Sid was pointing a finger at me to accentuate his question, but since I was semi-cowering behind the TV he seemed to be appealing to the set for the answer. Meanwhile I'd turned to our bookcases, filled with some one thousand books, all alphabetically arranged.

"What are you doing now?" he said.

"Put a leash on it, will you? I'm looking for a book. I want to read you something by Nietzsche that's very apropos."

"What? You think you're Zarathustra now?"

"I want to read you a goddamn paragraph of Nietzsche, Sid."

"Nietzsche, Nazi—what's the difference? I'm not buying into this either way, Vivian."

"Fine. Why are you so angry, though?"

"You're asking *me* a question. Let me ask *you* one: Where have you *been* the last few weeks?"

"That's not fair."

"What's not fair?"

"That little boy jealous tone. We agreed to leave that behind. It's embarrassing."

"OK, but you don't answer my question."

"You're asking me to defend myself?" My hand instinctively fell over my heart.

"I wouldn't mind an answer to my question," he said, simultaneously lowering his voice and raising his eyebrows. I paced a few steps away from him, toward the end of the bookcase in the corner.

"I've been keeping away because I've been feeling sad."

"What about?"

"Getting older suddenly. Feeling unattractive."

"That's crap."

"No, it's not."

"And what about me? I'm older than you and I've been unattractive my whole life."

"What are you talking about?"

"Five feet three and three-quarter inches, Vivian. I've never even been five foot four."

I looked at him and realized it was true. I was a good four inches taller than Sidney, but I'd never thought of him as being short. I mean, it never mattered to me. He was still thin; his eyes still had fire; and although there was a spreading bald spot in the middle, his hair was still a sexy blend of black and gray. Consequently, I was always shocked and saddened when he resorted to his height as a springboard for accusing me of some new infidelity—usually with Professor Galonzo of the Spanish department, who's built like a fullback and who'd admittedly always been friendly to me, though in a purely collegial way. Sid and I had wasted hundreds of hours discussing this obsessive fantasy of his, always followed by my reassuring him that it had never happened and never would.

"Sid, I thought we agreed not to keep things from each other."

"You've kept away from me."

"I had to think for a while, but things are clear now and I want to talk. I started this conversation, remember?"

"Very vividly."

"I didn't do it to depress you or threaten you."

"You know how I get when you start disappearing. How can I not feel it's meaningful when you disappear? I assume you're with the wondrous Galonzo, that lambada professor who's so obsessively fond of you."

"Sid, I was feeling sad and now I'm feeling better and I wanted to share that with you, that's all. It's something positive."

"Excuse me while I go to the bathroom and try to find something positive to share with you." He was trembling while he said this, his small, tight chest heaving a little. I knew it was best to leave him alone.

We stayed out of each other's way for the next two days— not an easy thing to do in a one-bedroom apartment, but years of adjusting to this sudden type of situation made it simple enough. Sid camped out in the recliner and ate his meals there, somewhat aided by a tray. I stayed in bed reading, resting and, alas, remembering.

Despite all the traveling that's supposed to exist in an academic life (and when I was younger I did travel, doing graduate work in England, Ireland, and France), I've somehow managed to end up in Brookline, the town where I was born. This apartment that I now own, I will probably die in—hopefully with Sid, and not because of him. All of this is to explain how easy it was for me to be attacked by childhood memories. I grew up in a house on Salisbury Road a mere half-mile away. Though I intentionally don't pass by the house, many of the stores and restaurants of my childhood, even the Coolidge Corner movie theater where I had my first double dates, are parts of my everyday landscape. Since my menopause, two childhood memories of my father have been persistently punishing me. This wasn't surprising, since he seemed to spend much more time

with me or at least to matter much more to me when I was a
child than my mother did. (Incidentally, though his personality
was strong, his body was weak. He died fifteen years ago,
whereas my bland and evasive mother lives on in Florida, calls
once a month, and gets a visit each Chanukah from Sid and
me.) In the first of these memories I'm ten years old, coming
in the door with a disappointing report card. I badly want a
hug from my father, and I want to see him smile when he sees
me, the way he smiles at me on my birthday, but when I walk
into his room, I see him sitting at his desk, consumed by sadness. I know it can't be because of my report card, which I
haven't even shown him and which only contains two B's among
a field of A's; yet I feel terribly, urgently responsible for his
condition. The other memory is closely related. My father has
dropped me off at a delicatessen to buy some salami and bagels.
There's usually a line in the store, but not that day, so I was
able to get the food and return to the car more quickly than
usual. I saw him sitting at the wheel before he saw me; again
immense sadness had spread over his face, mixed with a touch
of resignation.

It's impossible to describe how or why these memories hurt
me so much. I tried to filter them through Shakespeare, calling
on any number of his sonnets, including the one from which
Proust took the title for *Remembrance of Things Past*, but it
was no help at all. I began racing through my other channels—
scurrying through them like a rat—from Channel N (for
Nietzsche) to SAM, but nothing worked. Moreover, after my
memories of my father had their way with me, they were followed by a swarm of memories of my mother; then of my older,
more attractive sister I was always jealous of; and then of the
young girl who used to live in the apartment next door a few
years ago and who I used to sometimes wish were my daughter.
Memory Control was useless against this onslaught. I wept and
pounded my fist in my pillow until I felt dizzy. Then I cursed
Sid and God, possibly not in that order, and cried some more
before deciding to talk to Sid again. It suddenly occurred to

me that he really was in the dark about what was happening
to me.

Before I could actually begin, he sprang up from the recliner
and began pacing, clutching at his beltless gray pants to keep
them up. We made quite a contrast, him in his T-shirt full of
holes and me in my newly pressed blue print dress. I was also
wearing a fair amount of makeup for the occasion.
"I don't know if I'm ready to talk to you yet," he said.
"Are you still angry?"
"Angry was two days ago. Now I'm shaken, shaky."
"Please let me try to explain."
"What, about Memory Control? You know what that means
to me, you want to know what that all adds up to to me? You
want out, that's what."
"How can you say that! How can you even say those words?"
"You stay away from me for weeks, you tell me you can't
stand your memories. Who do you think you've had your mem-
ories with—Galonzo? I mean, should I feel encouraged by that?
Vivian look at me. I'm short, I'm bald, I don't make much
money. Like you say, I probably have a persecution complex;
I'm an aging, jealous, nasty little guy. Should I go on?"
"I don't want out. I've never wanted out. I've got to talk to
you. Sit down Sid. You have to listen to me this time. Sit down
in your television chair."
"I read here too, I don't just watch television like you say I
do. I'm not a moron, you know, just because I'm still an associate
professor. I often correct papers in this chair."
"Fine, then, sit in your reading chair or sit on the floor, but
just listen, OK?"
He ended up standing with one arm resting on the side of
his chair. He was going to give me my opportunity. I took a
breath.
Over the years my student evaluations have always praised
the thoroughness of my lectures, and I'm afraid that in the
beginning I gave Sid something of a lecture on menopause and
its effects on women in general. He didn't say a word, but the

hurt look was now fighting for space with an expression of concern. That helped loosen me up, so I began to tell him what it was all doing to me personally and how I knew I was being overly sensitive about my memories but that the Memory Control was just a mechanism I'd been using to try to control my pain and now it had broken down and I knew it couldn't help anymore. It had turned out to be an illusion and now I had no more control over my memories than I ever did.

"You're always going to have upsetting memories, Viv, just like you're always going to have regrets," Sid said softly. It was the first time he'd spoken since I began. I'd never known him to be quiet for so long. "I hope I'm not adding to them," he said.

"Of course not, silly. Weren't you listening? It was things from my past before you that were hurting me."

Sid made one of his humble shrugs.

"Is there something I can maybe do to help?"

Now I shrugged, inadvertently imitating him.

"Would you like to go to therapy?"

"I've done that."

"Would you like us to go to couples therapy?"

"We've done that, too."

He paced off a few steps and looked down at the Oriental rug my mother gave me after my father died.

"Would you want to maybe consider adopting?"

I forced a laugh.

"Oh Sid, you know we're too old. Besides, we're . . ." but I didn't finish my thought. I noticed he was smiling, almost from ear to ear.

"Why are you smiling?"

"Relief. I'd been thinking you finally got a good look at me and you saw this boney little Jew and were repulsed by me. Now I think, maybe not."

"Don't talk that way. On the contrary, I thought you were repulsed by me. I mean, these days I'm a sweating, nutcake mess."

Sid was still smiling, almost shyly now. "No, never, my beauty queen. That never happened. So, would it be in bad taste if at this dramatic moment I went out to get a newspaper? I'll be right back."

I gave him a funny look, wondering what he was up to, but said that it was fine, I'd be here when he got back. I knew he could only stand this kind of emotional intensity in little doses.

We embraced lightly. He kissed my forehead and I walked to his chair and sat down. Then I heard the door close. It was odd, but for a moment I felt like I did when my parents first left me at home alone without my sister or a sitter. Worrying that maybe they wouldn't come back, I'd construct all kinds of gruesome scenarios that would leave me an orphan. I buried my face in the chair where I could still smell Sid. Then I turned on the remote control and did some touring of my own until I settled on a PBS documentary on the Galapagos Islands, which proved to be pretty interesting. But I couldn't really pay attention, I was so edgy wondering what Sid was doing. Finally I heard the key in the door and I shut off the TV and jumped up from the chair. There he stood, sans newspaper, in his ripped T-shirt and baggy pants but wearing a bright blue spring jacket I hadn't seen him take when he left. He looked at me closely and I moved a few steps toward him.

"Look Ma, no newspaper. I wanted to be by myself for a little while and I have an idea now. You want to hear it?"

"Sure."

"You ready?"

"Sure, Sid. I'm ready."

"OK. Maybe it wouldn't be a bad idea if we got married."

"Are you crazy?" I said, but I knew he meant it. He suddenly looked like a very serious fifty-five-year-old man, and for a moment I felt sorry for him.

"You said you had a change of life. Maybe I've had a change of heart."

"Why now? Have you thought about this?"

"Better than thought—I've decided."

"Sid, we already *are* married, in effect. I don't understand why you want this."

"Maybe I want to make it harder for you to leave me if you find a better deal and I figure now is my chance."

I looked at him and made my own translation of what he said. After listening to me go on about my problems he finally felt equally attractive or unattractive and thought I was now as vulnerable as he was. It was the kind of painful translation I'd made before with Sid, which usually caused me to get angry or depressed and be all but defenseless against my memories of other men or of my childhood. But this time I felt something different. I felt calm and clear. No memories were assailing me. There was this aging man with very kind if somewhat sad eyes standing in front of me.

"Sidney, that's not a good reason."

"I know," he said, looking sheepishly toward his chair.

Suddenly I had a desperate urge to hug him and make him smile again, so I reached out and tapped him on the shoulder and held out my arms till we embraced. After a few seconds we said each other's names simultaneously and laughed at the coincidence; but instead of pulling apart, we continued to hold each other firmly in the middle of the living room. We had stopped laughing, but we had also stopped fighting. I had no desire to move.

Some Notes toward Ending Time

I'm sure Arthur Escher's recent death will promote an interest in his poetry and essays. His last book, for example, *Infinity Realized*, should be approved of by the younger generation, fascinated as they are with anything occult or even faintly exotic. As a fiction writer quite ignorant of philosophy, I long ago gave up trying to unravel his metaphysics. For me, Escher remains a vague series of idiosyncrasies that no doubt I understood as imperfectly as he understood mine. It's true my wife never tires of telling me that I knew him well, just as it's also true we once proposed marriage to the same woman. Yet there remains such a tiny part of him in my memory, it's almost as if he didn't exist as a thing in itself at all. But there I'm guilty of borrowing a term from philosophy, aren't I?

The point about Escher is simply that he spent so much time trying to dissolve reality through his time schemes, his Principle of Alternative Realities, his Categories of Collective Identities, that in the process he appears to have damaged the amount of reality he was given himself.

I would never have concerned myself with Escher except for the strange conviction of my wife, Julia, that I knew a good deal more about him than I was letting on. It all began about two years ago when I quite innocently made the mistake of asking her if she ever thought of Escher; at that point neither of us had seen him in at least seven years. Her eyes tightened to an expression of intense sorrow as she said, "The only thing

I really remember is he always wore purple—either a purple necktie or shirt or in winter a purple woolen scarf."

I didn't say anything to that. I was happy to let the matter die, but my wife began pacing our apartment in dismay that eventually turned to anger as she discovered that Escher (who had gone to the same university with her and even proposed to her, as she remembered it, on graduation day) had quite imperceptibly disappeared from her mind. First her anger showed in her extraordinary and minute criticisms of our apartment, which for years she'd decorated to her own satisfaction, and in which she'd regularly entertained with pride her circle of admiring or envious friends. Next she began to berate Manhattan in general, whose social excitements she'd previously extolled the way a good Catholic might praise his church. Then, inevitably, she took it out on me. At first I had no reason to connect her unfriendly behavior toward me with her feelings about Escher, but it soon became obvious. She began holding onto one of his books, quoting freely from it while she cleaned the house, hardly caring whether I was listening to its endless aphorisms or not. When she did talk to me it was invariably about Escher. As one might expect, her obsession grew in proportion to her insensitivity to it. How else can one explain the simple innocence with which she asked, "Why is it you never talk about Arthur anymore?" I looked up at her from my typewriter and saw her face open but strained, framed in black by a new severe hairdo. She was standing by the fireplace underneath a painting of the ocean.

"Darling," I said, "it's because I have nothing to say about him. I know no more about him than you do—in fact, far less."

"You're really incredible," she said, moving toward me. "Of course you realize you knew him before I did."

I shrugged and said nothing.

"You also realize that it was you who introduced me to him."

"Are you sure of this?" I said.

"What do you mean, am I sure? Are you trying to tell me that I have no memories of anything? It's you who can't remember anything. My name is Julia, can you remember that?"

she said as she stormed out of the room and abruptly slammed our bedroom door.

At this point I paused to consider my options. I'd been married nearly twenty years—certainly it wasn't a storybook marriage, but we'd learned to coexist in relative peace, with enough points of pleasure to get us through the years with our chins up. We'd rarely had any long fights, the worst being back at the beginning. She'd wanted to have children but eventually agreed it wouldn't be best for the kind of life we wanted. As for the scattered affairs I'd had, they were discreet and ephemeral—in the final analysis I was devoted to her. It wouldn't do to go storming out now or to go running in after her demanding an explanation. Julia had always been temperamental, even, at times, hyperemotional, and since she'd recently turned forty-five her hyperemotionalism had worsened. It was horrible to think about her in such a clinical way, but it was undeniably true: just before her forty-fifth birthday she began an almost militaristic regimen of dieting and exercising, along with a completely unnecessary preoccupation with her weight. Ironically, as she turned more jealous and possessive about me and more absurdly preoccupied with her weight, her interest in sex began to deteriorate. I was even starting to suspect her of an affair myself, though at that time (and for the last two years, in fact) I'd been impeccably faithful. Still, the question remained: Why should she suddenly be so concerned with Escher? Was this some kind of delayed regret that she hadn't married him? That made a certain sense; but how can you regret not marrying a man you can't even remember? And why drag me into the situation?

I knocked on the door and then walked in. Julia was sitting on the bed staring at *Infinity Realized* on the bed table.

"Julia, I'm very concerned that you've been feeling so upset about this." I was trying to adopt the quasi-fatherly tone that was often successful in placating her. "I'm also angry at myself for not realizing how much this apparently means to you."

Julia looked up from her book at me for the first time. In her eyes distrust and compliance seemed to have battled to a draw. Although it looked like she wanted to speak to me about it, she said nothing, and I tried to answer for her in my new gentle and fatherly tone of voice.

"Of course, looking at it objectively, it's the very essence of frustration. A person tries his hardest to make an impact—I'm speaking of Escher—he succeeds in capturing your attention long enough to become your friend, even to propose to you, and then simply because enough time passes you can't remember anything about him except an eccentricity in the way he dressed. That's sad for the person who wanted to be remembered, but it's sad for the rememberer as well."

Julia said nothing to this, but she did stay away from his book that night and allow me to kiss her goodnight on the cheek. By that time I'd arrived at the only obvious solution: to find out about Escher *for* her.

I'd begin an investigation in much the way I'd research a story, all in the hopes of constructing a convincing portrait of this obscurantist that would appease Julia.

Before I left the apartment for Research Day One I told Julia about my plans, but she was skeptical. She kept her head bent over the eggs on her plate and gave me mostly one-word responses.

"Not only will I find out enough about Escher to fill an encyclopedia, but if possible I'll bring him here to see you."

She barely answered me and kept doodling with her eggs, as if she were mesmerized by them, until I finally left for my mission.

For me New York is usually a network of pleasantly shifting sensations that keep me from fixating on any subject for too long, but that day the city seemed detached, the people on the subways and streets curiously frozen like paintings in a museum. Well, I'll certainly get nowhere if I start brooding over that, I thought, as I walked up the block to Gotham Book Mart. In a writer's directory in the bookstore I found Escher's address, which coincidentally enough was in New York. This was an exciting if potentially disturbing development. I tried to focus on the exciting part as I rode the subway once more to the Upper West Side.

At the apartment building on Riverside Drive a stooped, gap-toothed super told me that Escher had moved more than two years ago. According to the super, Escher was quiet, never caused trouble, and had a bad cough (could be the reason for his famous scarf). When I began pressing for more details the super looked at me sternly and turned away, saying he was busy. However, I didn't leave the building as I knew I was supposed to. Instead, I lingered in the lobby trying to engage Escher's faintly hostile neighbors in conversation, all the while enduring the dirty looks and supercilious stares of the super. From these neighbors I learned virtually nothing, so I went out on the road again. My next stop was the writer's organization P.E.N., where I obtained the name of his literary agent. It took a number of calls before her assistant allowed me to speak to Ms. Susanna Cotton. By then I'd made over twenty phone calls and taken more subways than I cared to recall, but I kept relatively calm on the phone, reminding myself of my wife's desperate need.

At last the dulcet tones of Susanna Cotton! Despite the rising tide of anger within me, I made the obligatory small talk before asking about Escher, only to have my hopes dashed again.

"I'm afraid Arthur's been traveling incognito in India for over a year now to research his new book. I get a postcard from time to time, you know, but I don't have a permanent address."

I looked outside the phone booth and noticed that the sky was dark except for a few clusters of blue the size of quarters. The day was over and I'd found out very little about Escher. Moreover, I had nothing to show Julia for my efforts. I started stalling to keep Ms. Cotton on the phone, inventing a ridiculously circuitous story that ended with my hinting that I might switch agents and have her, the wondrous Susanna Cotton (who had a reputation as both a viper and a dolt), represent me. That seemed to soften her up and allowed me to make my next request: Could I see her? Or better yet, since she was undoubtedly winding up her day, could she leave me a Xerox of one of his postcards with the receptionist? After all, Arthur was a dear friend and I was planning to see an anxious relative of his. Also, if possible, could she leave me a photograph—a publicity shot she might have on hand would be fine. Miraculously, for it is a miracle when something in this world works out, I got my wish. Armed with a four-line, faded postcard from India signed "Best, Arthur" and a publicity picture—a head shot of an undistinguished, barely smiling, undernourished-looking mystic—I returned to face Julia with a bit more confidence.

But things had gotten worse. When I opened the door I saw her washing dishes while reading a book of Escher's (*To Drown in Time: The Ecstasy of Oblivion*) that was propped up near the sink. Some kind of stew was cooking, but it was obviously an absent-minded affair.

"I spent the whole day trying to find out about Escher," I said.

"The whole day?" she said, without looking up from either dish or book.

"Yes," I said, nodding for emphasis and trying to resist the slight erection that her body in a navy blue dress still provoked in me. "You don't seem very impressed."

"I have trouble believing it . . . you," she said haltingly, the works aimed directly at the stew now, as if I were located there among the meat and carrots.

I felt, of couse, like throwing her across the room, perhaps also tattooing her head with the stew pot. But I kept quiet, controlled. Five minutes later she set the table, we sat down, and she began to stare into her portion of stew as if she were applying makeup before a mirror, an odd sight for a woman of impeccable manners. Then I noticed that she was crying.

"Julia, what is it?"

"Nobody remembers anyone," she sobbed. "I can't depend on you anymore, you'll forget me . . . soon I won't even exist."

"What are you talking about?"

"You only remember your stories. You'll forget me just like you forgot Arthur."

"This is crazy talk, Julia. Why would I forget you? I see you every day, you're my wife. And what does Escher have to do with all of this anyway? You treat him like he's your guru."

"He knows what I'm talking about. It's all in his books."

"Books, books, exactly! They're things he wrote to make money. Why do you assume . . . "

"Shh," she said, making a furious hissing sound that stopped me short. "I don't want to talk about it anymore. I'll stop crying now, but I don't want to hear you talk about him anymore."

A dinner-long silence followed during which my anger kept growing. But I practiced a kind of internal, yoga-like discipline and said nothing while Julia finished her meal. I even finished clearing the table, which I admit I wasn't in the habit of doing, while Julia retreated to our room.

The way things had been going lately I'd usually enter our bedroom late at night so that Julia could either be asleep or pretend to be. Along with the more obvious frustrations her sexual withdrawal had caused was the sheer awkwardness we'd feel around bedtime. This time, however, I walked in ten minutes after she closed the door. What should I see but my wife in a pale blue negligee through which her nipples were half visible, reading to herself from Escher's *To Drown in Time*, her lips forming each word like a child. It was possible she didn't even know I was in the room. To be candid, along with my other emotions, I now felt aroused.

"Julia."

She didn't acknowledge me but kept her head down over her book, silently mouthing her prayers.

"Listen to me. I saw his face."

"I don't believe you," she said softly, but with determination.

"No, it's true. You wouldn't let me tell you before, but I spent the whole day trying to find out about him, and I have a postcard from him *and* a photograph of him. I got them from his agent. I can give them to you right now."

She looked up from the book and stared off at the far wall.

"Even if it's true, and I'm not saying I don't appreciate it, what's a postcard to me, or a photograph?"

"I can't produce the man. He's in India researching a book."

I could see her shoulders tighten in the half-light of her bed lamp and the next thing I knew she slapped both her thighs, with unusually loud results.

"I find this all a little hard to believe, but it doesn't matter, you don't have to trouble yourself about it anymore. I'm going to hire a detective to find him. Out of my own money, don't worry. I've already contacted an agency."

I moved toward her feeling increasingly excited. "I think I've already been a very dutiful detective," I said, putting my hands on her shoulders, half anticipating that she might turn and slap me at any moment.

"You realize that I can't sleep with you," she said tersely, but not completely without mercy.

"Why is that, why must that be?"

"You want to destroy everything of mine, everything that's separate from you. You want me to forget everything about a man who almost married me. Meanwhile you have a habit of sometimes conveniently forgetting that you're married to me."

I felt a stab of terror, but since she hadn't formally accused me of anything, I decided to ignore the last part of her remark. Instead I withdrew the postcard and photograph from my jacket and handed them to her.

"Here, look at them. These are what I got for you."

She stared at them with an expression of such shocked fascination it was as if I'd handed her my entrails. Then she placed them carefully, side by side, on her bed table.

"I owe you an apology," she said, still unable to take her eyes off them. I noticed that her anger lines had disappeared and I felt even more attracted to her.

"That's just the beginning. I'll be bringing you much more. Forget the agency—*I'll* be your detective. I'll get to the bottom of this," I said as I reached around and squeezed her rear end. She didn't laugh at my pun, but she didn't stop me from continuing to touch her either. I did hear her whisper "You'll be my detective" a couple of times while we fumbled around, but by then I was too sexually stimulated to allow myself to take

offense. It felt like we'd been fighting for so long that I didn't
bring it up afterward either. Instead I did as I'd promised and
became her detective.

At least I did for a couple of months. And I did it seriously
and singlemindedly, as if I'd adopted a new profession while
casting my old profession of writing aside completely. I kept
logs, diaries, ledgers, phone numbers and addresses of possible
contacts, all of which I recorded carefully à la Joe Friday. I took
numberless train rides that screeched from stop to stop, while
others were gray, quiet, liquid, like being seated in a silent cellar
filled with water. At times when I can't sleep, which happens
at least every other night, I can still remember the faces of each
taxi driver I rode with, though other times they seem like different aspects of the same man.

I never found a phone number or address for Escher, but I
did determine that something about India beyond the topic of
his book had apparently kept him there. (Eventually he was to
die in India of a coronary thrombosis with complications, which
sounds complicated enough.) I did find more people willing to
talk about him. I found them through P.E.N. or through his
splendiferous agent and her army of assistants or through friends
of his neighbors. Each of them offered the dimmest of recol-
lections that had the quality of half-obscured footnotes. I often
felt that what little my informants told me was said out of
politeness or simply to get rid of me, so I never knew how
much was hearsay or even total invention. Nevertheless, I did
"learn" from them that Escher was modest, self-effacing, prone
to colds, undistinguished looking, perhaps a bit asexual.

Every night I reported my findings to Julia, but beyond those
strictly factual reports we never discussed the situation. She
remained morose and increasingly uncommunicative, though she
rewarded me sexually a couple of times a week for several weeks.
Then it dropped to nothing again. She had so little desire for
me that I simply became too embarrassed, and later too angry,
to touch her. To her credit, during our brief period of lovemaking
she did stop her refrain of "You'll be my detective," but those
episodes in bed were still strangely glacial. We were like two

figure skaters on seemingly parallel lines who only occasionally converge. As for our other times together, such as the dinners we still shared, we were polite but mostly silent. Sometimes when the silence became unbearable we'd talk about current movies and TV shows or else the news.

One night, after another futile day of detection, Julia met me at the door with a stare that showed no trace of recognition. Some time after that I arranged to move out.

In retrospect I see that I did try to salvage things; I even convinced Julia to see a therapist with me a few times. In a private session he told me that Julia had been deeply angry at me for a long time and that her obsession with Escher was her way of acting out the death of our relationship. By being her detective, I was probably acting out something similar. The whole question of sanity and obsessions is certainly a tricky one. A metaphysician, for example, might credit Julia with deep insight into our mental limitations and be quite correct. In the end one acts to save oneself, I suppose, so I ultimately stopped my search for Escher and filed for divorce.

Sometimes I recall a line from *Infinity Realized,* where Escher says that time is man's greatest vanity. Somewhere else he said that art forgets reality instead of reviving it. Once I began writing again, I must have realized that even a single story would help me begin to banish Julia and Escher and my peculiar relations with them indefinitely. With that modest objective I've written these pages.

Peacock Farm

It's June already. Milena's birthday is in a week. I don't know if she'll want to go out with me and her kids, or just with me, or whether she might simply like a present and not want to celebrate at all. I also wonder if she'll suddenly start feeling funny about turning forty. So far she hasn't said a word about it (any more than she's ever said anything about being five years older than me). I can't tell if it's because she's from Germany, where they're much less youth obsessed, or if she's just more stoic than I've realized.

I can already see the grass on the outer rim of the playground, less than three blocks away, and I press my basketball against my chest and make a muscle with my left calf. These last few years I've enjoyed checking on my suddenly more muscular body; I figure it's Nature's payback for my recently receding hairline. Then, against my better judgment, I break into a little trot. It's ridiculous how excited I get when the playground first comes into view. I start anticipating how many people will be playing and start imagining various scenarios. For example, that there'll be no one there—or, worse still, that a game will have started just before I arrive. I have a special horror of seeing that, so I usually try to get there a half-hour before prime time. On a Saturday morning that means 9:30 or quarter of ten, but today I got into this silly fight with Milena, and by the time we more or less made up I'd missed the bus to Harvard Square. Milena offered to drive me (I don't know how to drive) but I said no. I didn't want to deal with her while trying to psych myself up for the playground. Anyway, I knew she could never just drive me without some little controversy starting. With Milena everything has controversy potential.

It's embarrassing how seriously I take these games. If we lose and I don't play well, I'll often be depressed for the whole day; if the reverse happens, it can make my weekend or even my whole week. One time Gary, the guy I work with, went to the playground with me and we got into this two-on-two with a couple of high school kids. Almost immediately I went into my Charles Barkley/Bill Laimbeer hysteria, ranting and raving after every mistake either of us made and grunting on every rebound. Eventually Gary said, "Calm down, Cousy, it's just a game." Later he tried to discuss it with me in a Phil Donahue way, talking about male bonding and sublimating competitive instincts. I just laughed, mostly, because we'd won 21-18 and I was happy.

There are only two little kids on the playground shooting at the far basket. No one else. The playground stretches out gray and empty. I can't understand it. Then, when I start to shoot, I notice that a couple of clouds overhead look pretty threatening. So that's it: people don't trust the weather, and they want to see if it will clear off before they commit themselves to the playground. Except for two little kids. Little kids will come to the playground no matter what the weather.

After I shoot by myself for about twenty minutes the sky is still the same, or maybe a bit darker. One new little kid has come down, but one of the original two has left. Of course, most people my age on a Saturday morning in Harvard Square are working away on their dissertations or novels or having sex with their girlfriends. Although I'm concerned about money, I've never been that ambitious as far as careers go; as for sex, Milena would never do it in the morning, not with Marcus and Isabelle running around the house. There's a paradox here. On the one hand, she has this undeniable desire for me, but there are still certain things she wouldn't consider doing. Milena was raised as a strict Catholic and even spent some time in a convent. When we do make love she often blushes, and invariably she'll first go into the bathroom to change into an old-fashioned slip or dressing gown. Then she'll shut off the lights. She tries to arrange it, in other words, so that I never see her naked. Also, she has an irrational fear of smelling bad and will often drown herself in deodorants and perfumes. With all the lights off it's sometimes like making love to a smell. It's funny—she can be this disciplined, mature kind of mother during the day, but when it's time to have sex she suddenly becomes eight years old.

For some time Gary has been urging me to leave Milena, or at least to stop living with her. Just because she loaned you some money for the store doesn't mean she owns you, it doesn't make her your wife. Just treat it like a business decision and don't worry about her motives, he says. Gary owns the Xerox Shop in Central Square with me. We've only been in business a few months and there's a lot of competition. Right now we're losing money, although according to his projections we're supposed to for a while. I admit it's a really good oportunity, but I'd feel better if I could begin to take some money home.

After I shoot for about five more minutes I realize there's not going to be any game here today. People around Harvard Square are pretty picky about their playing conditions, I guess. There's a bus to Lexington that I could catch in fifteen minutes, so I decide I'll leave as soon as I make my last three shots. For about a year now I only leave the playground after I've made two final jump shots and a lay-up. Today I feel a little weird, though—my concentration isn't right—so it takes me a while to make them. As a result, by the time I get to the Square I've missed my bus, and a minute later I'm on the phone to Milena. Talking to her on the phone is never easy, partly because her English isn't that good.

"Hi. I'm coming home but I missed the bus, so I'll be back in an hour and a half."

"How was your basketball?"

"Basketball is over. That's why I'm coming home."

"But it rains soon. I come to get you."

"I can stay out of the rain."

"I meet you in front of The Coop in twenty-five minutes, OK?"

"Sure," I say.

And like clockwork she is there exactly when she says in her station wagon, her cheeks red, her green eyes huge and comically overfocused as she looks for me. I can see Marcus and Isabelle in the back seat. It's Marcus who finally points me out, just before I wave to them. Then Isabelle lowers her head and pretends she can't see me, while Milena smiles from ear to ear. My first feeling is, I'm really glad she brought the kids. Their father is Iranian, a rising star or possibly already a risen star in the physics department at MIT, and the kids, especially Marcus, have his dark hair and swarthy skin. But Isabelle has light hazel eyes, and neither of them are smarmy the way he's supposed to be.

While we ride, Marcus, who's six, asks me a lot of questions about basketball. Isabelle, who's eight, looks out the window feigning disinterest, though she chips in with a question or joke every five minutes or so. Milena has an inscrutable expression on her face, which means she's probably thinking about her husband. I feel a little flash of pain. I guess the way her marriage dissolved is pretty typical. At first they were close, then Farhad got career obsessed and started neglecting her in bed. This made her bitter, especially since she was kind of an aristocrat in Heidelberg and went against her family's wishes in marrying an Iranian. The next thing she knew he started making moves on their maid. Milena immediately kicked Farhad out and sued for divorce. He, in turn, moved to Cambridge and now sees his kids once a week. He's refusing a divorce by postponing things and trying to negotiate with Milena. With Farhad, everything's a negotiation. But he's very strong willed under the mousy front. I met him briefly before he really knew who I was, and he did seem reserved and even soft, but somehow scary, too. This happened a year and a half ago. I've been living with Milena for a year now. We live in a large brown ranch house a couple hundred feet off the expressway that goes to Cambridge, on Peacock Farm Road. She has a big yard where I often play

Whiffle Ball or hide-and-seek with Isabelle and Marcus. In the yard today I see a Frisbee, a Whiffle Ball and bat, a croquet mallet, and a rocking horse. Like all kids, they litter toys.

After Milena puts them in front of the TV, in which she doesn't believe but on which she increasingly depends, she goes into the kitchen and starts slicing celery and potatoes. She's making a potato salad for lunch, keeping her broad back turned to me, waiting for me to remember the fight we had this morning and say something soothing. The fight was about our relationship—more specifically, about her suspicions. ("Why do you run away from me? Is is really basketball you're playing?") We met at an adult education class in Cambridge where, in her own awkward way, she picked me up. At the time I found it pretty appealing. Her fumbling aggressiveness struck me as innocent and touching. Even when she began mothering me, at times, I felt touched. Here is someone you can trust and turn to, I said to myself. Her heart is still as pure as her children's. You won't get double crossed by this one like you have before. At a certain age, it's just too wearying to be lied to. So when she started buying me gifts and writing me love letters (with every third word misspelled) I was charmed. And when she offered to help me financially I felt a little guilty and nervous, but (since I needed it) grateful and flattered too. So I went along with that, and with the idea of my "temporarily" moving in with her because my one-room apartment was "so sad and pitiful" it broke her heart to see me living there. I knew her wounds from her husband were still fresh, but I thought, This one is guileless, this one is kind.

We slept together pretty quickly, which might have contributed to her suspicions about me; I don't know. During the fight this morning I asked her what could make her doubts go away, and she said marrying her. I reminded her, as I often do, that she still is married. I further reminded her that she's profiting quite nicely from the separation and might not fare as well from a divorce. I also said I didn't think she really wanted to divorce Farhad. "But I hate him much more every day, Danny." "But you also love him," I answered.

It went on in its usual circles like that. At the end of the fight Milena started drinking wine and I went upstairs to call Gary. Once again he asked me point blank why I'm staying here. I said, "I don't know; I guess I must love her. Anyway, my feelings for her kids are really intense." He said, "In what way?" and I said, "I'm afraid of losing them." When I got off the phone my hands were shaking. That's when I decided I'd had enough introspection for the day and it was time to play ball.

Milena still isn't talking. Although I think of her as high strung, when she wants to she can be infuriatingly patient, as if she doesn't have any nerves at all. The only sign of tension I see in her now is that her shoulders are slightly hunched up, like a porcupine's, and that every minute or so she flicks some thin yellow hair away from her ears.

"Why don't I take the kids for a swim before lunch?" I finally say, right after I notice that, perversely enough, the sun has broken through, and there will probably be basketball games all afternoon. She turns and smiles. She loves it when I do stuff with Marcus. She constantly tries to throw us together. However, I suddenly remember that Marcus probably won't want to go because he got stung by a bee near the pool yesterday.

My suggestion causes fifteen minutes of pandemonium, Marcus crying, Milena imploring, Isabelle running. When everything settles, Marcus stays to watch TV. I've promised to play catch with him alone after lunch, and I leave for the pool with Isabelle. Peacock Farm's pool (owned and regulated by Peacock Farm's residents) is in a cleared-out part of the woods. A trail that starts at the end of Milena's yard will take us there in five minutes. Once you set foot on the trail, however, the woods become very thick and the house soon disappears from view.

I let Isabelle walk ahead of me. She is one of those paradoxical-looking children who has a sensual and an angelic aspect to her beauty and whose thin little face is both friendly and mysterious. For some reason I can't resist letting her get farther ahead of me; then, crossing off the path, I run through the woods until I get ahead of her again, where I can hide behind a big oak tree. I see her pink feet walking over the dirt trail,

time myself, and then jump out laughing and screaming. She
jumps back a step and screams herself—three little screams that
sound like echoes of my own. Her face hovers between laughter
and tears. Finally she lowers her head like a tiny offensive
lineman and charges into me, swinging her fists the whole time.
I duck most of her punches but one or two hit me in the chest.

"Why did you do that?"

"It was just a joke."

"Why did you try to scare me?"

My first impulse is to say, "Why did you hide in the car when
you saw me in the Square this morning and then pretend not
to see me?" But I stop myself.

"I thought you'd think it was funny. I'm sorry."

She has that conflicted look in her eyes again, but after another minute of explanation she decides to accept it. I end my
apology with a florid appeal, asking her to forgive me.

"Yeah, forget it," she says. That isn't the response I'd hoped
for, but she's already turned on her pink-slippered toes and
starting climbing the stairs that lead to the pool. Then, before
I can get acclimated to the pool situation, she takes a one-step
dive and is soon moving rapidly from side to side, at the outer
limit of the area she's allowed to swim in, like some kind of
sleek pink fish. By "the situation" at the pool I mean those
Peacock Farm residents who come to spy, gossip, occasionally
flirt, or just test their status. And there are people in our neighborhood with some serious status: two Nobel Prize winners,
various government officials, and a half-dozen bona fide mil-
lionaires. Today Mr. Dalrymple, a commodities player, looks
intentionally mysterious in his sunglasses as he reclines on his
favorite chaise longue at the far end of the pool. Only last
Saturday he chewed my ear off about the private life of our
Nobel laureate in physics, who's his neighbor. Ten minutes later,
after I'd excused myself and joined Isabelle in the pool, he
stopped me as I passed by. "Where's Marcus?" he said, pointing
at Isabelle still frolicking in the pool. "Home with Milena" came
my perhaps too quick reply. "He has a little temperature."

"You're very fond of Isabelle, aren't you?"

"I'm even more fond of Milena."

"How lucky for her," he said. My heart was pounding. I didn't like either of our answers.

"But I think *I'm* the one who's lucky," I said, recovering fairly nicely, I thought.

I was still nervous and stayed to talk some more. I couldn't tell if he was onto my thing about Isabelle. I wasn't sure what my thing for Isabelle was myself, except that it wasn't the right way to feel about children. Eventually he tried to do some research on me. I had to lie about my résumé and tell him that I'd graduated from a college out West (when I didn't quite graduate from junior college) and that I got the startup money for the store from a business I sold there. (I have solemnly promised Milena never to tell anyone about the money she gave me.)

Today I decide to preempt Dalrymple by giving him a long coast-to-coast wave, which he's finally forced to acknowledge from the other end of the pool. Then I shift to phase two of my plan and withdraw my own pair of black-rimmed sunglasses from my shirt pocket. I put them on and sit back two chairs away from Mr. Griffin, whom I greet with a nod. I don't have to do more than nod discreetly at Mr. Griffin; I've only talked with him once. It's his wife, Inga, who I know better. She is German and a great friend of Milena's, although not a great enough friend so that she didn't once try seriously to flirt with me. In her youth, according to Milena, Inga was an ardent Nazi. It was Griffin who rescued her and brought her here. He is nominally a professor but in reality has worked many years for the CIA. He is alcoholic, impotent, and dangerously in love with Inga, who, at fifty-seven, is still beautiful and still cheats on him shamelessly. One does not really want to do more than nod at Mr. Griffin.

Well, this has become a day of shattered plans. I certainly won't be able to swim with Isabelle today. I'll be trapped into playing catch with Marcus later, and now I'm trapped in my seat between Griffin at one end and Dalrymple at the other. There's nothing to do but stare and occasionally wave at Isabelle, who may still be angry at me for scaring her.

Suddenly I close my eyes and try to summon up a memory of Gary giving me one of his Free Yourself from Milena speeches—specifically the concluding part, where he lists all her deficiencies. "She's neurotically jealous and possessive yet frustrates you in bed. She doesn't really understand you or even what you say half the time. She's got a crazy husband and she's insensitive to your feelings. Remember when she introduced you to that woman who was a Nazi and thought it was a big joke? Not even considering how you might feel, being half-Jewish."

I open my eyes. It isn't working, because I'm upset about what I did in the woods with Isabelle.

One day, shortly after I moved in, I went to Marblehead with the three of them. Isabelle sat in my lap all the way back in the car. She kissed me at least ten times that day, and I became terribly excited in spite of myself, though I'm sure she didn't know it. Now she already shies away from contact with me. Soon I'll only be able to kiss her on birthdays and holidays. That's also something you're supposed to accept, like being too old to be chosen for basketball pickup games. The world is very sure how these things should go, but I'm not. If it were up to me, I wouldn't have such rigid boundaries around everything, such clear résumés that are supposed to please everyone.

Isabelle has gotten out of the water and is spending a lot of time wrapping a towel around herself as if it's a fur coat. Finally she walks halfway toward me and says, "I'm going home."

"OK. Me too."

I jump up from my chair and exchange nods with Griffin. Dalrymple, meanwhile, keeps his head behind the stock page, although it's impossible to tell whether he is reading or watching me.

On the path back I walk ahead of Isabelle and turn my head every time I talk to her.

"Did you have a good swim?"

She nods.

"It was fun watching you. Did you see any fish underwater?"

She half smiles and shakes her head no.

"How about mermaids? Did you see any of them?"

This doesn t get a verbal response either. She lifts her eyebrows to convey sarcasm.

"Are you still mad at me for scaring you?"

She shrugs, then mumbles no.

"Can we kiss and make up?"

She shakes her head no, in one fluent, definitive motion.

"I think Milena would be really upset if you told her I scared you. I think it would ruin her day. Did you know she has a birthday coming up, that it's practically her birthday? I hope you don't tell her."

Her eyes stare ahead blankly, as if she didn't hear me or wasn't paying attention. The sun looks fractured now. The whole sky is cut up into ragged patches of gray and blue.

Milena has set the wooden table outdoors. She can't resist a picnic; it's the European in her. When she sees me she starts running at me. Apparently she's already upset.

"Thank God you're back! Marcus is crying ever since you left. Why do you leave him out so much?"

"Where is he?"

"Under his bed. He won't come out. You must play catch with him Danny, you must! He worships you."

"All right, I'll do it after lunch like I said. Calm down, OK? I'll go get him."

Marcus doesn't exactly worship me (with Milena things often have religious connotations), but he does like me and listen to me. He's under the bed all right, but I treat it as if he's playing a game; I tell him I'm a hungry wolf dog coming in after him, and as soon as I start barking he starts screaming and slides out from under the bed in a flash. I catch him as he comes out and give him a ride all the way downstairs while he squeals with laughter.

Lunch is another matter. Isabelle keeps her head turned away from me the whole time while Milena drinks wine and reminisces about her dead brother. Marcus keeps bothering me and soon my stomach begins acting up, so I postpone our game of catch until later in the day. I go into my room, shut the door, turn

on the Red Sox game, and for a couple of hours am able to
tune everything out.

Suddenly Milena bursts in, without knocking of course
(though, in fairness, it's her room, too), with a tortured look
in her eyes that I've seen a thousand times before. I lie back,
head propped up by two pillows, and continue to watch the
game, holding the remote control firmly like it's a glove I'm
wearing in the winter. Milena paces around the room, sits down
on the bed, gets up, paces again. I get to watch two more
batters before she steps in front of the TV.

"Danny, please, you must talk with me now, will you?"

"What's the problem?"

"Why do you jump on little Isabelle like that?"

"For Christ's sake, I didn't jump *on* her, I jumped *out* at her."

"She is so scared. She is shivering when she tells it to me. It
is so pitiful."

"It was a joke, goddamit. I told her that. Look, I'm getting
sick of being cross-examined, I haven't done anything wrong.
I'm getting sick of everyone's precious sensitivity."

"Where do you go now?" Milena says as I start to close the
door. "Danny, where?"

"I'm gonna play catch with Marcus so you won't yell at me
for not doing that. I'll see you later." I finish shutting the door
and run downstairs. Marcus is watching a war movie.

"Come on, Marcus," I say, turning off the TV. "Get the red
ball and your glove. We're going to play catch."

He looks stunned for a second, but I've said the magic word,
so he tears off for the kitchen, where he keeps his glove. He's
wearing blue shorts and a rather effeminate peach-colored T-
shirt that Farhad bought him.

"Danny, I can't find the red ball. Can we use the Whiffle
Ball?"

"No. It's time for you to start catching a real ball."

"But I can't find the real ball."

"Did you look under the couch in the living room or behind
the TV?" He runs out to look for it. Marcus loves to play catch,
but the thing is he catches like a cymbal player who, time after

time, can't make them hit squarely. What happens is Marcus will smile for a while, but then he'll feel humiliated and start to cry.

I walk into the kitchen feeling kind of strange. Milena, who is usually an impeccable housecleaner, has left the dishes in the sink unwashed. My eye goes to the little scraps of food that Isabelle always pushes into a neat pile on the side of her plate. I think, I shouldn't have done what I did. Ever since that car ride back from Marblehead my feelings haven't been right about her; but still, I haven't really done anything wrong, and I certainly never will. I pick up the silverware from her plate and then my mind kind of goes blank for a moment. When I focus again, there's blood on my hand. Marcus comes running into the kitchen. "I can't find the red ball anywhere. Danny, what's the matter?" he says, his black eyes opening wide.

"I cut my finger washing the dishes. Go upstairs and get me the Band-Aids from the bathroom cabinet, OK? And don't disturb Milena 'cause she's resting, all right? Run quietly."

He sets off almost as quietly as I'd hoped. Christ, what a pair we are! I'm cutting myself with a knife, and he's still trying to catch his first ball. While the faucet's running I realize that this game of catch will never work, especially with Milena (doubtlessly) watching from behind her drapes the whole time. Then I remember that the Fleischmann's house at the end of the road has a basket in the driveway. They're still in Europe on their vacation and said I could use their basket anytime I wanted. A couple of times when I was really desperate I'd shot with Nat Fleischmann in his driveway, so it wouldn't be a problem. Also, Marcus could learn something new without the pressure of Milena spying.

I hear him running before I see him. He's almost out of breath as he hands me the Band-Aids.

"Is it still bleeding?"

"Don't worry, it'll stop." I put on three Band-Aids as carefully as I can, although I'm rushing as I do it.

"Hey, Marcus, I got a good idea while you were away. How'd you like to play basketball with me?"

"Basketball?"

"Yeah. Did you ever shoot a real basketball at a real basket?" I open the hallway closet where I keep it and hold the ball out in front of his hands. "See? It's a much bigger ball than a baseball. Feel how big it is." Marcus smiles and looks up at me. "It's as big as the world," he says. I laugh and explain to him (while writing a note for Milena that I'll leave by the door) that we have to take a walk before we can shoot the world-sized ball.

Outside it's completely clear. The sunlight is so strong that I feel dizzy and the sky is a bright blue. The court in the Square is probably jammed by now, or will be soon, but I don't mind. In fact, I feel strangely peaceful. Marcus, meanwhile, is dribbling the ball semi-spastically all the way to the Fleischmanns.

The Fleischmanns live two houses away from Dalrymple. When we get there I look around for signs of him, but I don't see any. Fleischmann's basket has one of those half-moon white backboards that I hate, and I try to explain to Marcus about the size and shape of glass backboards. The basket is about twenty feet from his garage, with maybe twenty more feet of level black pavement behind us before it slopes out to the road. I keep wishing we were farther off the road but I feel good anyway. I shoot a few layups, a short hook, and hit my first few medium-range jumpers. Of course, Marcus is easily impressed. He claps and cheers and practically does a somersault after every basket I make. I realize that he's perfectly happy being my caddy and hasn't even hinted that he'd like to shoot. Then he starts trying to catch the ball after every basket I make, before the ball hits the driveway. He's only successful at this a few times, but whether he catches it or not, he eventually runs with the ball and hands it to me wherever I'm standing. After about ten of these trips I start to feel bad and realize it's time to change things.

"OK, now you're going to shoot," I say, holding the ball. He looks confused for a moment but then runs up to me and takes the ball with both hands. His first seven shots fail to hit any part of the basket.

"I could do better if there was a glass backboard," he says. "Forget the glass backboard," I say. "You've got to aim higher, that's all. Throw the ball way up."

"How high should I throw it?"

I look up at the sky and the sun floods into my face. I tell him to aim for the top of the backboard and he nods, as if I've made an obviously sensible suggestion. He shoots his next shot with both hands after a running start and makes a tiny grunt when he releases. The ball brushes against the net and maybe grazes the bottom of the rim.

"That's better, that's real good," I say as I catch the ball. He smiles tentatively and looks a little surprised as I bring the ball to him. "We'll just stay here till you make one," I tell him, as I walk back beneath the basket.

I watch a few more of his shots, but then my mind circles back to the woods and Isabelle, and then to Isabelle on my lap in the car sneaking in kisses while Milena looks out at the road. I figure as long as I know they're just images that happened once and won't again, it will be all right.

"Danny," Marcus says, wondering why I've been holding the ball for so long, "can't we keep shooting?"

"Sure," I say, throwing him a soft bounce pass that he fumbles away. "I've got nowhere else to go."

Song of the Earth

After his phone call to Perry, Ray let out a little scream and jumped with raised fists, slightly bruising his knuckles against the wooden beams. Then he ran around turning on every light he could find, for the trees were thick and so near the windows that the cottage was already dark and chilly. He thought of trying to start a fire to surprise Joy when she got back from her run but he doubted there was enough time, so he fixed himself a drink instead.

When Joy returned, Ray was finishing his second whiskey sour. While she toweled off by the fireplace she told him a long joke about a couple she'd seen at the beach; he pretended to laugh but took advantage of the moment to study her. She looked amazingly good. She was thirty-five, his age, but he thought she looked younger than he did. She'd always had what he considered a classic female figure except for her unusually broad shoulders, which, coupled with her height (she was only an inch or two shorter than he was), at times gave her appearance a forbidding quality. Yet when her long blonde hair hung down straight, as it did now, her shoulders were tremendously exciting; the more he thought about it, they were exciting regardless of her hairstyle, perhaps just because they were so dramatically incongruous in her otherwise gracefully proportioned body.

"Did you speak to Perry?" she said, stretching her legs out as she spoke. She was wearing her navy blue running suit.

"He invited me to his home tomorrow for lunch."

"Wow!" she said, springing forward as her face exploded into a smile. "Congratulations! You're going to have lunch with Perry Green! What a coup!"

"Take it easy. It's not as if I've just won the Pulitzer."

"I'd say you just took a big step toward winning it. Perry Green is probably the only legitimate triple threat in music now that Bernstein is dead, except for maybe Lukas Foss. He's one of the most prominent conductors of modern music in the country. He's definitely one of the most influential critics, and he must be on eight zillion juries or boards of directors."

"He's also a famous composer. You forgot that."

"That too."

"No, not that too. As far as he's concerned *that's* his real identity."

Joy nodded uncertainly, as if barely able to repress another joke.

"Yes siree buster, I'd say it's a coup. It's working out just as you'd hoped."

"Do you think you can drop me off there tomorrow?"

"I'll do better than that. I'll make you dinner tonight if you'll promise to tell me all about the fast society you're running with these days."

Ray smiled and said it was a good deal. She made chicken crepes, broccoli and carrots, and tapioca pudding—all his favorites—and he told her an edited version of how he had met Perry Green. There was a party of musicians in the Village, what he had thought would be basically a bunch of composers his age kvetching and consoling one another. He'd heard a rumor that Perry would be coming but hadn't fully believed it until he saw him, looking slightly frail in a pale blue suit and yellow Windsor tie, by the punchbowl in the center of the loft. Then it was simply a matter of screwing up his courage (a vodka tonic helped him there) and striking up a conversation.

"What did you talk about? Did you tell him you had an

old girlfriend who once sang in one of his song cycles at Tanglewood?"

Ray laughed and said he would tell Perry all about her tomorrow. At the time, though, he had thought it best to steer clear of shoptalk. Instead they'd talked about books and movies and New York politics—although they did talk about Perry's book in progress, on Stravinsky's ballets. Ray barely mentioned that he was a musician, much less a composer. But it worked, or something worked, and Perry suggested they have lunch, which they did a week later in the Village. Then they talked more freely about themselves, and when they discussed summer plans Perry said he'd be at his house in Tanglewood and invited Ray to visit. Ray hadn't thought Perry meant to invite him to *stay* at his house, so he had thought of calling Joy. And now here he was, tremendously in her debt.

He stopped talking to finish his drink and saw something unsettling in Joy's face. Had she assumed that there was more to the story? For Perry Green was rumored to be a homosexual and was often seen with men thirty or forty years younger. Was it that, or something else from her own agenda? Quickly he offered to introduce her to Perry and she said that would be great.

"Of course, I should have made that clear to you earlier. Actually, I meant to tell you when I first called that you could benefit from this too."

"Not to worry," she said, but that anxious expression was back in her face. Ray watched her closely. Maybe it had nothing to do with Perry and she was instead concerned that he might make a pass at her now. Over the years they'd both worked at becoming friends who could joke about their past relationship and still do occasional favors for each other. Yet here they were, in her cottage in the country. Neither was involved with anyone else, and it seemed they'd never gotten along so well.

"I'm getting really tired," Joy suddenly announced, before yawning with exaggerated emphasis. "Will you need any help fixing up the sofa?" He said no; she wished him good night, and as quickly as he had envisioned the possibility it was removed from him.

"Who are you staying with?" Perry asked. They were sitting at a white patio table shaded by a white and blue umbrella sprouting from its center.

"A woman named Joy Davis. We're just friends," Ray said with a wave of his hand. "She's a teacher and singer who sang in the chorus of your 'American Song Cycle' actually, at Tanglewood a couple of summers ago."

"Really? Did she drive you here?"

Ray nodded. "I wanted to introduce her to you but she turned shy at the last minute."

Perry chuckled and adjusted his sunglasses. "I have a friend staying with me too—the young man who brought us our drinks. His name is Bobby. You'll have to talk to him later. He's delightful."

"What would we do without friends?"

"Indeed!" Perry said, still laughing. Then he fell silent until, just as Ray was about to compliment his yard, Perry asked the magic question.

"Tell me what kind of music you write. I'm sorry I'm not familiar with it."

"There haven't been many performances of it in New York. And, of course, no records yet. But I keep plugging away. It's tonal, mostly. Some might call it neo-Romantic, though I don't like the label."

"Labels are for librarians. They call me a Romantic too, and a conservative. But I think I'm kind of a wild man, wouldn't you say?"

"Sure," Ray said. Then, after Perry began laughing, he laughed too.

"I hope you brought a score for me to read."

"I have some back at Joy's house. A short symphony I've just finished and a string trio I'm working on."

"Splendid! You'll have to bring them to me tomorrow, or tonight if you can come over."

"Really?"

"Of course. Bobby will fix us all dinner. He's an excellent cook."

"Thanks so much."

"And bring Joy too. I'd like to meet her."

"She'll certainly be thrilled to meet you," he said, immediately wishing he hadn't been so florid. He reminded himself that he was succeeding by staying in the background and letting Perry orchestrate everything.

Between four and five, Perry went in the house to take a nap. He'd invited Ray to use his guest room but Ray told him he'd like to stay by the pool and maybe swim again.

"It's so exciting to be young," Perry said. "All that wild energy." He laughed a little, then walked down the steps in a careful, almost stately manner (not unlike the way he approached the podium when he conducted) before disappearing into his house. Ray had gotten up from the chaise longue and was watching the house from the diving board. Perry was definitely playing some kind of game with him, but what was it? First he was the relaxed but dignified host. Then he seemed to show a possibly jealous interest in Joy; yet a moment later he invited her to dinner. Of course, he had asked him about his music and offered to look at it, but was that said out of mere politeness?

Perry was certainly a master of mixed messages and as a result, he'd kept Ray off balance all day. The nadir of the afternoon had to be when Bobby, after serving them lunch, sat down to join them. It turned out Bobby was not merely a waiter but a sometime actor. Perry's bright blue eyes sparkled as he talked about Bobby's auditions. Was this his way of demonstrating that he had no vulnerabilities in his love life? Yet Bobby was also naive, bordering on goofy, and not particularly attractive. He even had a fairly substantial case of acne. It was true that Perry was somewhere in his sixties with thinning hair, but he was still Perry Green, and on stage (albeit with his hairpiece and elevator shoes) he was an imposing figure. At Tanglewood, Joy said his poster sold better than ever.

For several minutes Ray had been walking from the diving board to the patio table and then back, turning every few steps to look back at the house below. On one such trip he stubbed his toe near the table, swore out loud, and then sat down in a chair, telling himself to calm down. He inhaled deeply a few times and watched a pine needle drift over his head in the light breeze. Above him the cloudless sky was a deep azure. When he was young and came to Tanglewood with his parents he used to call them Mahler skies. How inexpressibly beautiful it was to hear Mahler's Resurrection Symphony or "The Song of the Earth" under such a sky across from the tree-lined lake. Of course Tanglewood was much more built up now, and more businesslike. He could never feel about Tanglewood (or even about Mahler) the way he did twenty years ago.

Looking down at the pool he remembered the most stunning event of his afternoon with Perry. They had gotten up from their seats to go swimming. "It's a little obscene to have a pool here, I suppose," Perry said, "but I often feel too tired to bother with the lake." Then they went into the water together, laughing while they waded.

"Look at our feet," Perry said, pointing below the water. "They look identical. That must mean we're twins."

That moment in the pool was the closest Perry had come to flirting with him. But was it serious flirting? And if it was, and if Perry persisted, what would he do? He knew one thing: He would call Joy before she left for Perry's and ask her to bring his scores with her. He was going to put them into Perry's hands tonight.

That Joy chose to wear probably her best white cocktail dress might have worked, but with her long turquoise earrings, her pearl necklace, and gold and turquoise rings, she looked top-heavy and garish. She'd even worn twice as much eyeliner as usual, and a fat smear of red lipstick. It was immediately obvious to Ray that she'd tried too hard—a big mistake in dealing with Perry. Moreover, she talked too much and too loudly about all the wrong things.

Perry, of course, remained unflappable. He allowed himself to be interviewed about a bevy of subjects Ray thought indiscreet, and he complimented Joy a number of times on her appearance, as if hoping his praise would have a tranquilizing effect on her. Meanwhile, Bobby, acting preoccupied with his dinner, said nothing but was unfailingly able to laugh whenever Perry made a joke or laughed at one of Joy's.

For the first half-hour Ray tried to contribute some comments of his own in the hopes of slowing Joy down. When this failed, he concentrated on drinking wine and staying silent. It was only shortly before they left (while Joy was in the bathroom) that Perry turned to him and said, "Did she bring your scores?"

"Yes. I have them in my briefcase, actually." He went on to say that he would greatly value any comments Perry might make. Perry removed his glasses and smiled at him as he took the scores, while Ray tried not to stare at his wrinkles.

"Are you free to come for a swim tomorrow before you leave?"

"Sure," Ray said.

"Say twelvish?"

Driving back, Joy sang bits of various arias, mixing in dirty jokes and laughing continuously. He could never tell at such times if she was truly happy or just projecting an elaborate cover.

"Isn't Perry amazing?" she said once they were back in the house, as she again made up the couch for him.

"He's very nice."

"Now I can die and go to heaven, I've dined with a great man. Aren't you happy too? He said he'd look at your scores, didn't he? God, what an opportunity."

"I'm pleased," he said with a tentative smile.

"I should think so," she said, putting a hand on the hip of her white dress. "Haven't you gotten everything you wanted?" Their eyes met and he felt she was looking at him meaningfully, as if he could sleep with her. He was excited too, but something froze him. Instead of trying anything he yawned and let the moment pass.

But he couldn't fall asleep. He felt vaguely as he had years ago, the night before his master's exam. It was the knowledge that something momentous would happen tomorrow, for he was certain that Perry would look at his work before they met for their swim. Regardless of what he thought, Perry would have to say something positive; but what he said would hardly matter. It was really a question of what Perry would or wouldn't offer to do to help him, and then, of course, what Perry might expect in return.

He thought of Perry's own music, buoyant, crisp, and civilized. It was also romantic but always controlled. Might Ray not expect reasonably controlled conduct from him too? He reminded himself that Perry was over sixty and had complained about his heart. Perhaps he merely enjoyed flirting and wouldn't want anything too drastic to happen right away. Of course, Perry could just as easily make a pass at him tomorrow and end by asking him to do something unthinkable. He didn't really know Perry and could hardly predict his behavior. But what would he do if something did happen? He had never had sex with a man and there were certain things he knew he couldn't do, especially with AIDS around, when sex with men had become like Russian roulette.

He tried focusing on the question of just what he would do with Perry but found it excruciating to think about. Instead he started thinking about the look in Joy's eyes that night, her long blonde hair and big shoulders. It was odd, but he'd wanted her more than he ever had during their relationship. Why had he turned away from her? Was he already punishing himself for his thoughts about Perry?

But maybe it wasn't too late. If Perry Green could champion his music, anything was possible. He turned on a dim lamp by the couch, put on his slippers, and walked to her room, the floor creaking with his every step.

"Joy," he said softly as he tapped twice on her door in the near total darkness.

"What's up?" she said matter-of-factly. "Come in."

"Me, obviously. I'm having trouble sleeping."

"Sounds like the Ray I know."

"Were you having trouble too?"

"Me? No, I'm too uncomplicated to be an insomniac."

"Sorry. I guess I'm disturbing you then."

"No problem," she said, her voice still even and toneless.

"Can we talk for a few minutes?"

"What's on your mind?" she said, turning on a bedlamp before he could ask her not to. Her face looked strained in the light, as if it were fighting against something, and he thought she was keeping her eyes on a point just behind him while she talked.

"I guess I'm nervous waiting to hear what Perry will say tomorrow."

"Don't worry, it'll work out. Why wouldn't it? Your music's good, he seems to want to help people he cares about, and he certainly cares about you, don't you think?"

Something in her tone stung him. It was one thing to be sexually rejected by Joy (which she'd all but made clear by now) but quite another to be put on the defensive like this.

"I think he cares equally about you. And you certainly showed the whole night long how much you cared about him. I've never seen you so enthusiastic."

"I don't get your point, Ray."

"There's no point. It's just that I never knew you could flirt so relentlessly."

"That's a strange thing to say. God, Ray, I don't know that I appreciate that. It seems a little hypocritical too, under the circumstances."

He felt his heart pound and took a step back toward the doorway.

"How's it hypocritical?"

"I didn't leave my scores with him."

"You're not a composer."

"I didn't leave my business card either."

"So what are you saying? That it's a sin for me to try to help myself? That I shouldn't show him anything and should just be a meek little music teacher the rest of my life and never get anywhere?"

"I'm saying I think you're maybe accusing me of something you're doing yourself."

"And I'm saying you're maybe a little jealous." He shut the door—he didn't think he slammed it, but it made an inordinately loud noise. By the time he reached the sofa he already regretted it and realized he should apologize. But how? It suddenly seemed an incredibly difficult thing to do. What was happening to him that it was so hard to say he was sorry? He had always considered himself direct and spontaneous, but now he was becoming so ineffectual, so Hamlet-like. Was it this Perry business? Or maybe it had really started years ago, when he moved from Somerville to New York. But that was too painful and ridiculous to think about. In Somerville he had been a child with no conception at all about how careers were made. Somerville was about long afternoons at the piano, summer trips to Tanglewood, and dreaming about being the next Mahler. A movie a few years ago had shown how Mahler converted to Catholicism to help his career. Was it true? Even Mahler probably wasn't what he seemed, and had had to put in his New York years as well.

Ray walked across the living room and again knocked on her door. "I want to apologize. You've been exceedingly generous to let me stay here, and I was a pig to say what I said."

"I'm sorry for some of the things I said too," she said, once more in a matter-of-fact voice that gave away nothing. "Why don't we get some sleep and I'll see you in the morning?"

But in the morning her face had only softened a little and that maddeningly neutral voice was still intact. Moreover, she continued to avoid his eyes, something she used to do years ago whenever he had disappointed her.

In the car on the way to Perry's he thanked her profusely and she smiled. But when he asked her to the concert and proposed a farewell dinner afterward, she quickly found a reason why she couldn't do either. He felt so discouraged that he lied and told her that Perry had offered to give him a ride to the bus station so she needn't call for him. Then there were some awkward words, a tepid kiss on the cheek, an inscrutable and probably forced smile on Joy's face before she drove off, leaving him at the iron gate to Perry's house.

"This is ridiculous," he said out loud when he discovered that the gate was locked. It took him a confused minute or so to ring the buzzer, and another few minutes before Bobby emerged in a pair of madras shorts and white T-shirt to let him in. He had his characteristic smile that Ray alternately saw as either innocent or empty. After he opened the gate, he shook hands with Ray effusively. "I'm going into town to do some shopping for Perry."

"To Stockbridge on foot?"

Bobby giggled. "I need the exercise. At least Perry thinks so." He began his high-pitched quasi-hysterical laugh, which Ray determined to cut off with a question. "Which store are you going to?"

"A lot of them, practically all of them. He has very particular tastes. I'll be gone for hours, but I guess exercise is a good cause."

"Well, if I'm gone before you come back, good luck to you."

His smile faded. "I'm sure I'll see you soon. Oh, by the way, Perry's in his room. He asked if he could meet you there."

"Sure," Ray mumbled.

"You can get in the house from the back." Bobby waved and smiled again, then began whistling some innocuous tune as he headed down the road.

Ray walked up the stone steps cut into the front lawn, then circled around the left side of the house, where there were alternating gardens of petunias and tiger lilies. In the backyard he stood on tiptoe to view the pool, but he could see just a sliver of water before he was in the house. For a moment he wondered which way to turn until he heard Perry's voice.

"Ray, is that you? Keep turning left and then left again." Perry was sitting at his desk arranging papers. It was a bright, airy room filled with photographs on the walls and dominated by a large unmade bed against the far wall. Perry rose from his chair and shook Ray's hand warmly, asking him to sit down on a green velvet chair just behind him.

"You can see I didn't quite make it to the pool yet."

"Did I come too early?"

"Not at all. You're as precise as ever. I just went a little overtime on my book. I'm writing about the opening of *Orpheus*. It's kind of silly to try to put it in words, don't you think? The whole book may really be kind of silly, but I'm supposed to be a champion of Stravinsky. The Stravinsky Society even gave me their medal," he said, pointing to his wall where it hung between autographed pictures of Koussevitzsky and Copland.

"Say, you look even more glamorous today than you did yesterday. I love your pink shirt, especially with those sleek black bathing trunks. And your sunglasses make you look so mysterious—like Marcello Mastroianni."

Ray laughed a little, then took them off. "It is silly wearing them inside, however," he said.

Perry studied his face. "Well, maybe you're right. You do have such expressive eyes that you should never hide them for long, though right now you look a little anxious. Would you like it better out by the pool?"

Ray shrugged, too boyishly he thought.

"I think so," Perry said, still pointedly studying him. "I'll change into my suit then if you don't mind."

"Of course not," Ray said. He kept his eyes fixed on the photograph of Hindemith, resolving not to look at Perry for a second as he fumbled out of his pants.

"I looked at your stuff last night. Seems pretty interesting to me. I like the flute against the drums in the waltz section."

Ray felt his heart beat again as he waited to hear more, but all he heard was the sound of Perry changing clothes. Finally he said, "Thank you."

"You look a little sad, but now that I know you're a composer it makes sense, I suppose. That's a good enough reason to be sad."

Ray turned and looked at him. Perry was wearing a baggy navy blue bathing suit and a white polo shirt. He looked short and a little shriveled. At least he doesn't try to look young, Ray thought.

"May I keep your pieces a little longer so I can try to understand them better?"

"Of course."

"I get the feeling that I've disappointed you somehow. I hope not, of course. I liked a good bit of what I saw."

"Oh no. I'm very grateful. Anything you say means a lot to me."

"Tell me the truth, Ray. Do you really want to be a famous composer?"

"Only if my work deserves it."

"That's a good answer. The problem is so many people think their work does. It's curious why people chase so hard after public fame when they can make *each other* feel famous so easily."

"How do they do that?" Ray said. He could still feel his heart, but everything else in the world seemed to have receded from him except this conversation.

"Why, through love, of course. But people hold back so stupidly. It's a tragedy, really."

"But you're famous. You're famous all over the world. Are you the exception to the rule?"

"I never expected it. I did hope for it at a certain time in my life, and I did do things to help my cause, but I never compromised myself, I don't think. At least not too badly," he said laughing. "I haven't, at any rate, been as lucky in my pursuit of private fame. I think you have a much better chance of getting public fame than I do of getting my private one."

"Why's that?"

"I think it's very obvious why. You're young and crushingly handsome and you have drive and talent, and I'm getting older, my energy's petering out, and I just feel my chances dwindling all the time," he said, looking deeply, almost incriminatingly into Ray's eyes, as if begrudging him his relative youth. "Let me ask you another question, Ray," Perry said as he took another step toward him. Ray had gotten up from his chair as well; they were now standing a few feet from each other in the middle of the room. "Do you think of your life as a challenge or a disappointment?"

He thought of Joy and of his tiny apartment on the Upper West Side. "Both, probably."

"Touché. Well then, do you consider yourself disappointed with your life so far? That's a better way to put it."

He felt then that he had never loved anyone happily, never accomplished even one of his career goals.

"It's fair to say I'm somewhat disappointed so far. So where does that leave us?"

"How rare are absolutes attained, how valuable are compromises," Perry said smiling. "You see, I've always believed the way to avoid disappointment is not to expect absolute victories in either work or love. Take solace in small victories whenever you can. You can believe they're real, at least. That's why they call the other fantasies or dreams."

Ray stopped himself from making a joke about Perry philosophizing so much. Instead he said, "But you've gotten so much success, you've realized your dreams."

"Ah, you can't be too sure about what I've gotten. You'd have to know what I wanted first. For instance, I'm not going to get you the way I want, am I?"

Perry's lips trembled as he asked his question. Ray stared with fascination at them, and at the moisture that had gathered above his upper lip.

"No, I guess not."

"And maybe you had hopes that I could make you famous, but I can't. It's really beyond my power. So much for absolutes. On the other hand, I could lend a hand here and there, help you out a bit every now and then. I think you're very bright and just tremendously attractive."

"And what could I do for you in light of what I just said?"

"The pleasure of your occasional company is the main thing. Small things. No absolutes. Can I, for example, give your back a massage now?"

"Here?"

"Don't look so mistrustful. I mean literally what I said. A backrub, that's all. Just lie down on my bed. You don't even have to take off your shirt if you don't want to."

Ray looked up for a moment at the rows of autographed pictures before he walked toward Perry's bed. Every time he thought he'd seen them all there'd be a Shostakovich, a Casals, or a Heifetz he hadn't noticed before. It was as if these were magic walls perpetually revealing the images of new musicians.

When he lay down he tried to understand what he was feeling. He decided he was anxious and slightly angry—nothing he couldn't control. He closed his eyes and tried to imagine they were a woman's hands, perhaps Joy's. Then he tried to think of analogous situations, how baseball trainers routinely rubbed the arms, shoulders, and backs of their players. But this didn't work either, and his eyes stayed open the rest of the time.

Perry's touch was surprisingly strong and skillful, and so far he was sticking to the rules. "These hands have played duets with Heifetz and Hindemith," he said softly. "You shouldn't find them so repulsive. On the contrary, you should find them at least somewhat interesting. After all, they can make a hundred men sit down and play beautiful music. How does it feel to have them rub your back?"

Ray said nothing. He was certainly not going to say anything that might excite Perry, but if he stayed silent much longer he worried that he might seem too passive. "You're very good at it."

"Ah, and I'll get better yet. You'll see. You merely have to tell me what you like and I'll adjust."

For the next minute the only noise Ray heard was his skin being rubbed. It sounded like the lake lapping up against the sand. Then, without warning, except for his slightly heightened breathing, Perry broke the agreement. His hands began moving down Ray's body without the slightest hesitation. Ray wanted to say something, but the longer he waited the more impossible it became to speak. Finally he said, "Just be careful, I have to insist on that. Just promise you'll be very careful, OK?"

The Horror Age

Shortly after I turned eleven, I found out my mother was seeing another man. This was no secret I discovered, since my father and she would yell about it to each other, along with other subjects (like his drinking or lack of money), about three times a day. The idea of my mother cheating on my father seemed both disgusting and faintly exotic. I tried to imagine becoming a woman who could do it, but I couldn't, because I'd always end up feeling sorry for my imaginary husband. For a while I thought of her as a kind of prostitute, though I also somewhat admired her as well. Then I finally stopped thinking about it after they were divorced.

Given the nature of my mother's crime, which she never denied, and her obvious guilt, I wasn't surprised at what happened next. My father was in my room hovering over me as tall as a building. I never knew how tall he was and thought of him as a magician who could change his size at will. I looked up at his inscrutable face.

"Thea, your mother's moved out. She's left us alone just like that. You'll be staying with me now. You'll get to see her on certain days, but don't ever worry, you're my daughter and I'll never leave you. I'd rather die than leave you, you understand?"

My mother moved all the way to California with her new young man, then later to Mexico. In the next year I saw her four more times, each visit more awkward and bitter than the one before. From these visits I found out that she was angry at my father and me and at life itself. She was a nervous woman and a nervy woman who wore bright dresses and red lipstick that almost matched her fire-red hair, and lots of perfume, though she didn't shave under her arms. These are my last images of her. Almost a year from the day she left us she died in a car accident in Santa Barbara. She was drunk and alone (her young man had left her) and I'd always suspected she'd committed suicide. I don't remember crying much, but I remember my father crying, which made me angry. He'd fondled me a number of times that year, and I was often angry at him in those days.

When I'm alone in an apartment for a stretch of time I can easily slip into the annoying habit, which I'm slipping into now, of brooding about my past like a Tennessee Williams character (one of my favorite writers, by the way). I've been alone in my new apartment for two hours and fifteen minutes now and, true to form, I've been spying on my past again. This is how I wound up in this situation. I had left three apartments in New York, my father each time taking the train up from Philadelphia to talk about what went wrong. Then, after a day or two of working with an agent, he'd pay the security deposit and two months' rent for a new apartment and then arrange for the movers to get my things so he could personally move me in. During these visits I'd stay in a good hotel with him because, after what I'd tell him about my apartments, he couldn't rationalize allowing me to stay in them one more night. While I stayed with him he was polite, though a little stilted. (The incest stuff hadn't happened for fifteen years). As soon as I was moved in, of course, he went straight back to Gail, his very serious girlfriend.

What went wrong in the apartments? In the first one, in Chelsea, there were drug deals going down next door, among other things. It was ridiculous. The next one, on the Upper West Side, was riddled with bugs—cockroaches, waterbugs, bugs that flew. Plus some maniac kept playing his trumpet at all hours. Finally my father sprang for a one-bedroom apartment on the Upper East Side. It was safer, but by then I was losing the point of being in New York. I had worked in a travel agency, in an art gallery, and at a university bookstore. I couldn't stand the jobs, and I couldn't stand eating out in the restaurants, or cooking for myself in such a small kitchen. As soon as I'd come back from work I'd find myself daydreaming a lot.

This time my father decided I absolutely had to leave New York. (I admit that going there in the first place had been my idea, my conviction, my demand.) He'd had it with New York and wouldn't finance my next apartment unless I lived near him in Philadelphia. There was no argument from me (though I was sure Gail wouldn't be thrilled). I couldn't offer a single argument in favor of New York. It would be like trying to defend the Holocaust.

So what did my father come up with this time to reward his only child for her brave move back to Philadelphia? The moment he opened the door to this place I turned cold. My father was smiling. His gray eyes were suddenly alive and sparkling. It wasn't a fake smile, but who knew what it meant? He told me to walk in and look around, reminding me again that this time he hadn't relied on real estate agents but had picked it out himself. I walked through the kitchen and living room and spent a few moments more than I wanted to in the bedroom. I hated it with a hatred beyond anything I'd felt for any of the other places. I couldn't say this, of course, though his eyes were demanding a response. I sensed he needed a word from me so he could feel he'd done right and could go back to Gail with a clear conscience. Meanwhile, to stall a little, I walked back into the living room.

Some places burn you and some places freeze you. This one was definitely a freezer. I felt like I was being led to my execution, but when he asked me how I liked it I said, "It's nice." I could say this because technically it was the best apartment I'd had since I left home. It was clean, there was enough space, everything worked. The living room and bedroom even had windows that looked out on the Schuylkill River, so it was a believable thing to say. My father smiled, clicked his heels, and headed to the door. Then, just as he turned to go, as if he'd remembered a water faucet that was still running, he turned and gave me a hug. Mostly I felt the outside of his gray winter coat. For some time he's been quasi-phobic about touching me. Better late than never, right? Except that sometimes I do actually wish he'd hug me or give me a morning kiss. Don't get me wrong, I've never forgiven him for what he did, especially for the fact that he never admitted doing it. But my father and I have spent a great deal of time together. He taught me how to ride a bicycle and how to swim and cook. He sent me to camp and private school and two colleges. He's a difficult man, and when he gets too tormented he can obviously do desperate things. But he can also be charming and smart and know how to make me feel incredibly cared for. Crazy as it might sound or be, I've never found anyone else I could really love, at least not for any length of time.

So here I am in my new apartment, lying down on my bed with my coat on. I close my eyes in an effort to sleep but a moment later I get this strange feeling that I'm lying in a coffin, so I open my eyes and keep them focused on the window, which from my position only shows a blank line of sky. Finally I'm able to calm down.

From my father's point of view, there's nothing to not be calm about. He's even arranged another job for me, after first allowing me a month's rest to "settle in." It's a secretarial position in a public relations firm. That's his field, public relations (the irony isn't lost on me), and he has many connections in the city. He's become quite successful. My father's is one of the most dramatic and magical career comebacks I know of. I've often wondered whether my mother still would have left him if she could have known what lay in store for him. Of course, I've also wondered what she would have done if she'd known what lay in store for me. (I had thought about telling her, and once, while we were at an outdoor restaurant in Santa Monica, I almost did. I guess I didn't because I was afraid she'd become pointlessly hysterical without doing anything about it, that she'd merely use it to yell at my father from 3,000 miles away. My father, in turn, would find out I'd betrayed him about something he never admitted had happened in the first place.) Sometimes I think no one is as clever as my father. Maybe Houdini was, with all the impossible traps he escaped from, although even he finally failed. Still, my father comes closest, which is why I picked Houdini as my secret nickname for him. Over all, it fits.

I guess I'm thinking about Houdini a lot because I've picked this day to ask him some important questions, and to really try to get some answers from him. I know that lots of other times I'd thought I'd do the same thing, but this is a truly special day. It's my return to Philadelphia, thus marking my official failure in New York. No day could be more appropriate. If all the possible days when I thought I would do it were spread over me like stars, this one would glow brightest and my eyes would go right to it. In other words, if I don't do it now, I never will. Basically all I need is some kind of reasonable plan, though I can feel that percolating inside me too. Yes, today Houdini's number may really come up.

It's gotten colder, amazingly cold for November. I look down from the sky and press the red heat button onto high. Heat blasts into the room. Finally, a decision not to be an icicle! While I'm on something of a roll here, I wonder if now might also be a good time to call someone and announce my existence, but I don't really have any close friends left in Philadelphia. Even as recently as three or four years ago I had a little society of dynamic people, but almost all of the dynamics have left for New York. (And, of course, I also went to New York.) Then, with all the trouble I had with my apartments, these former friends got harder to keep track of and more or less disappeared.

I remember a key conversation I had four years ago with one of the Philly dynamics named Shelley who I felt might become (and she actually now is) a therapist or social worker in New York. We'd had a few drinks at a quiet place in Center City called The Wine Bar, and for some reason I'd told her a little about what went on between me and Houdini in my sordid past. Shelley had listened really closely and winced a couple of times to show empathy. It was quite touching. Her nose also

had a peculiar way of crinkling as if she were trying to identify
a smell she couldn't exactly place. At the time she hadn't known
what to say. It had impressed me that my story had made her
speechless; now I know it was because I was so vague about
the details. But, not knowing that then, I had plowed right
ahead to my next topic.

"What's really difficult is the graduate student slut he's sleeping
with these days, who's more or less moved in." I went on to
detail the peculiar horrors of Gail, who, as it turned out, began
living with my father a month later. It took me quite a while
to get it all out, since there are a lot of awful things about Gail,
some blatantly (objectively) awful, others subtly awful, others
awful because of my particular situation; so it all required a
lot of careful explanation. After I was done, Shelley finally
spoke.

"The thing with your father must be really painful, you know,
since it's so ambiguous."

I pounded my fist down on the table and the glass jumped
a little like a jumping bean. At least I think I pounded my fist,
because it was so uncharacteristic of me that it was hard to
realize I did it. I remember the absolute silence in The Wine
Bar, the bartender staring at me like the foreman of my jury.

"It *isn't* ambiguous! There was nothing ambiguous about it,
because it really happened! He touched me in some bad places
and made me touch him, not just once but about seven times.
OK?"

Then Shelley's whole face crinkled and she let out a weird
little gasp—more like the sound an insect would make than a
human. This was followed by profuse apologies, mutual reas-
surances, and eventually a flow of tributes from both of us.
But we could never talk about it again, although indirectly
Shelley tried. She told me that my whole life lay ahead of me.
I said I wasn't so sure, but that now that I thought about it, I
judged my life to be pretty enjoyable in a lot of ways. Shelley
didn't say anything to that. She was busy telling me that I was
beautiful and smart and still really young, all of which I naturally enjoyed hearing. We were both twenty-three then and

agreed there was nothing major to worry about until twenty-seven. That was the horror age, the age by which you had to have it together with men and careers and whatnot. I have to smile when I realize my twenty-seventh birthday is in three weeks.

Thinking about how sincere Shelley was makes me wonder why I didn't get in touch with her once I moved to New York. Actually, I did call Shelley once in New York. It was shortly after I left my second apartment, on West End Avenue. I left a message on her answering machine but she never called back. Maybe the message didn't register. That's the thing about answering machines; you never know about all the messages that didn't register, and the people who leave them can never be sure (since the machines are so fallible) whether their messages are heard or not. It's a lot like praying. Were you heard? There's no way to know. Of course, I could have called Shelley again, but I took it as a sign that my message wasn't meant to be heard by her. I guess I'm the kind of person who always sees signs in everything.

As I'd suspected, it's gotten hot in the apartment. Leave it to Houdini to pick an apartment with a lethally overactive heater to cook me in. Burning and freezing, one extreme to another—how typical of him! For Gail, it's doubtless very exciting ferreting through all his contradictions and extremes. That's pretty heady stuff for a just starting out therapist who's only five years older than me. How Gail would react to my story if she knew it is another thing. I used to fantasize that, in a proverbial moment of weakness, Houdini might have told her. Now I know that's impossible. How could it have happened? Would it be after they'd just finished having intense sex and while they were holding hands in bed? He'd say in a hoarse whisper, "I want to tell you something that's been on my mind for a long time, darling"—*very* unlikely scenario. Or say they were out to eat at a restaurant (Houdini loves to take Gail to restaurants) and while they were sipping champagne he'd say, "I want to unburden my heart to you about something that's deeply troubled me, Gail. Fifteen years ago, I nearly lost it with my daughter."

No it never happened, it would never happen. Unless, naturally, I were to tell Gail—but then Gail would dismiss it out of hand, unless, of course, I were to befriend Gail first—but that's the most ludicrous fantasy of all.

I've been pacing the last few minutes, starting to feel that I'll either freeze or burn here, that getting out might actually become a matter of survival. Now I remember that on the way over Houdini invited me for Thanksgiving, still almost a week away; but he also invited me to visit anytime I wanted. So it wouldn't be totally ridiculous if I went there now, though it would be disconcerting for Gail, who'd certainly have a frown or two behind her red smiles. Lately Gail has had lots of reasons for smiling, too. I'm sure she's going to marry Houdini soon; somehow his moving me back to Philadelphia is connected with that. But should it all be so easy for him? Couldn't he have a word or two with me first? It would be a mistake to call ahead, though—that would only give him time to prepare. If I totally surprise him, the odds of his talking to me will increase dramatically, regardless of what Gail says or does. And Gail would be less prepared too.

With this in mind, I suddenly leave my burning/freezing apartment. In Houdini's house it always seems to be 72°.

My enthusiasm didn't last long. No sooner was I outside than I started to debate whether to walk or try to take a taxi. It was certainly cold enough to take a taxi, but I didn't want to arrive too soon. I felt I needed a little more time to figure out what I wanted to do once I got there, so I ended up walking through the killing cold, regretting that I hadn't worn another sweater. Then I started worrying about how I looked. I admit that many people have told me I'm pretty; I've enjoyed it and benefited from it throughout my life. But I also feel that I have the kind of face that never really changes no matter what I do with my hair or makeup. The only thing that changes is sometimes I get the feeling that my eyes have wandered away to stare down at me from some distance. Other than taking these mystical leaves of absence, my eyes are steady and hazel. Gail, on the other hand, is able to greatly alter and usually improve the way she looks by varying her eyeliner or lipstick, thus keeping Houdini a little off guard and constantly aroused. She's also the most elaborately casual dresser I've ever known, with different pairs of slightly faded jeans and clinging T-shirts for every occasion. It's past five and the streets are already getting dark and drained of pedestrians. Houdini's house in on Lombard Street over a mile away. It's a roomy three-floor house, quite tastefully done, and it would be worth millions in New York. But looking at it, and knowing that it's in a not especially glamorous part of Philly, you can't tell what the house or its owner is worth. (Thus Houdini strikes again!)

Before I even walk up the porch stairs I can see them through the living room window where the shade is only half down. It looks to me like they're conspiring and I feel like turning around and heading back. What would I say to them anyway? What could I say to Gail? "I see that you're wearing a blue dress. I see that time is still happening to you." Then I remember that they often look like this whenever I happen to see them before they see me, so I climb up the porch steps on tiptoes. Everything is suddenly still. Sometimes when it was quiet like this I used to think the stars were acting as silencers, the sky's police keeping everything silent and under control. It was one of the things I used to believe as a child.

I knock twice on the door. Gail answers and her smile leaps on her face like a flame. For a while I can't speak, I'm so mesmerized by the smile; that seems perfectly balanced on her face, like a figure skater. I search it closely for signs of overt phoniness or malice, but I can't find any. Meanwhile, Gail is already talking to me while I watch her blue eyes shining with joy or some other kind of excitement.

"What a nice surprise," Gail is saying. "Harold, come quick! Thea's here."

Houdini appears, looks at me for a split second with a half-smile. Then his eyes look down. Nervous, definitely nervous. Something isn't right here, with my appearing like this. After all, I can be counted on never to do or say anything important can't I?

"Come on in," he says.

"Yes, hurry on in, you look frozen," Gail says. "I'll get some tea."

I walk into the living room after Houdini, who stoops a little because of his height. He sits down and his legs stretch out endlessly like garden hoses.

"How's the place working out?"

"It's nice. I like it. It's real roomy," I add, just to be a little more convincing. He smiles and nods while he waits for Gail. He doesn't seem to have much to say. He fidgets. Then Gail comes with the tea and immediately starts asking me questions. How is my apartment? Am I looking forward to my new job? How do I feel being back in Philadelphia? It's often Gail's method to ask me such questions, especially after I first arrive. That way she can convince Houdini, and even try to convince me, that she's genuinely interested in my doings. I don't warm to these questions, of course, because they all point to my substandard accomplishments. I was obviously not a screaming success in the workplace, was obviously not able to stay in any of my New York apartments for more than three months and had returned to Philadelphia for these very reasons. So what was I supposed to say? Nevertheless, I mumble some "appropriate" (one of Gail's favorite words) answers and Gail cocks her head to feign interest, the way people cock their heads when they talk to a dog or parrot. Houdini continues to look somewhere between uncomfortable and depressed. I look at him while Gail babbles on, and I remember that it was he who told me that stuff about the stars keeping things on Earth quiet. He used to tell me things like that when he'd read me stories, and he used to read me stories a lot. It's strange to think of that, and it makes me feel kind of shaky. I ask if I can have a drink and Houdini says of course and uses the opportunity to disappear. Once he's gone, Gail apparently sees no purpose in continuing her concerned-therapist shtick, so she suddenly stops talking and I look away from her until Houdini comes back.

When he hands me the glass, a shiver goes through me. I realize how cold I am and drink the whiskey sour as quickly as I can, while letting them talk to each other for a while. Then I stand up and say, "I'm gonna get myself another drink. OK?"

"Sure, Thea." Houdini says, with his quizzical half-smile.

In the kitchen I start thinking about drinking. I didn't think he ever took drugs, so I'd always assumed he drank before he touched me. Although I could never remember him drinking much, I assumed he must have done something to forget who he was, or at least to alter his head. Yet I couldn't be sure. It was something I had always wondered about. At any rate, during my own nymphomaniac phase I drank my way through it. I remember wanting to see if it *was* possible to have sex and completely forget the person, and what you did with them. But I could never succeed. There was always a little something— an image, or a word I'd remember. The last time was three months ago and I drank again, which made me aggressive and weird and probably scared the hell out of the college kid who was doing it, who thought he had picked me up in a bookstore.

Just as I'm planning to leave the kitchen I see Houdini fidgeting again, which he often does in the company of the two women in his life. I think he's become increasingly nervous with age. It's as if he's always thinking, "Time is speeding up. At this rate . . . I'll die." These days the only way he really relaxes is by watching as much sports on television as possible. If he was being candid he'd have to admit he couldn't get through life without ESPN.

I finish my second drink in the kitchen, then immediately fix myself a third and carry it back to the living room. He and Gail are drinking tea but he can't seem to keep his eyes off my whiskey sour.

"Want me to get you a drink?"

"No, I'm fine." As if to prove it, he and Gail conduct some small talk for the next few minutes—just bantering away about nothing, while she sips at her tea.

"So when are you two getting married?" I say.

Houdini looks embarrassed but Gail clings to her professional
I'm-empathizing-with-your-feelings face.

"That's personal," he says.

"Personal. Hmm, let me see if I understand. Personal like
one's private parts—that kind of personal?"

He looks at me for a second, then says, "Excuse me, I'm going
upstairs." A publicly announced escape—Houdini has crossed
me up again. Now I'll be alone with Gail to boot. I stand up
and watch his long legs lightly float upstairs, out of sight. Gail
still has her patented, deeply concerned expression in her eyes.

"Are you OK?" she says.

"Yes, I'm fine." I look at her. I can feel the alcohol making
me stronger. "No, I'm not. I want to talk to my father about
something." I take a few steps.

"Be gentle. He's had a rough day."

I look directly at Gail, who suddenly turns her head away
modestly, like a Japanese woman, and for a moment I'm sure
she knows.

"He worries about you a lot," Gail says. I want to say, "I'll
bet," or something else sarcastic, but instead I freeze and don't
say anything. "And he loves you very much."

"I'm going upstairs now. Excuse me," I say. I wasn't going to
discuss my father's love for me in front of Gail.

I find him on the top floor in the attic, staring out a large
oval window that overlooks Center City. Beside him a radiator
hisses. The whole house is heated by old-fashioned radiators,
for technologically he's retrograde and likes things at least fifteen
or twenty years old.

At first I stand still, waiting for him to turn. Then I realize
that he hasn't heard me or else is pretending not to. With his
back to me and his arms suddenly extended against the attic
window, he looks like an image of the crucifixion. His new
dramatic pose convinces me that he's heard me, but still the
bastard magician doesn't turn around. Finally I knock a little
louder than I need to against the half-open door.

"Thea," he says, his arms collapsing till they fuse with his
hoselike legs.

"Who else?"

He looks at me carefully. I get the feeling he doesn't like what he sees. His eyes look nervous.

"What's up?"

"I wanted to talk to you."

"Shoot," he says, pointing one of his hoses vaguely at the door, which I then shut behind me. I pause for a second to remind myself how much I've drunk and to remember that I'm stronger now.

"Sorry if that crack about getting married embarrassed you . . . or her."

"No problem." He's still looking at me with infinite expectancy and wariness.

"I was just curious and blurted it out. But, anyway, are you two tying the knot? Is that the plan?"

"Could be. It could be in the cards. Is it all right with you?"

I walk farther into the room with a series of big strides and circle him a couple of times before stopping. Then I make a point of forcing him to look right in my eyes. "Me? No, it doesn't bother me. You've been together so long it's hardly surprising. And you say you love her, so it's only natural that this would eventually happen." I stop to catch my breath, while he looks at me like I'm a top spinning out of control that he wants to pick up from the floor. Then I say, "You and Gail are fine. What's not fine is *my* life."

"What's wrong with it?"

"You don't know?"

"Not unless you tell me."

"OK. I'm having trouble feeling motivated lately."

"And?"

"I guess I'm not getting along that great with men. I know, I've had lots of boyfriends, but it hasn't added up to anything."

"Why not? You certainly don't have any trouble attracting them."

"I have trouble trusting them, or when I try to trust them I feel haunted, like there's another person in the room watching, waiting to reclaim me for some reason. Though what could it be?" Houdini persists in looking puzzled. "Dad, do you remember what happened the year Mom left?"

"It was a very bad year. It was hard on all of us."

"Do you remember what happened with you and me?"

"You're losing me, Thea."

"Do you remember some strange stuff going on between us?"

"No. Except I drank way too much that year. I saw a psychiatrist that year."

"Yes, I know. Therapists have done a lot for you. Look at Gail."

"It was just a tough time, Thea. Best forgotten, don't you think?"

"You don't remember anything else? Like touching me in the den?"

"What are you talking about?"

"Specifically, putting your hand on the crotch of my pink shorts? And also squeezing my breasts."

"That's nonsense. That's rubbish!"

"And that was only one time, Dad. There were others. A number of others. In my room at night when you tucked me in, and in your room in the morning, and once on the front porch when you were supposed to be reading to me and you made me touch you too."

"You've been drinking too much, Thea. You don't realize what you're saying."

"No, I'm not drunk Dad. We both know it happened. We both know." I can see his eyes narrowing while his face is turning a kind of seashell pink.

"What do you want from me? I can't tell you it happened when it didn't. A man would have to be a monster to do that to his daughter. A man who did that wouldn't deserve to live."

He looks at me. He's as close to crying as I've seen him since the night my mother moved out.

"What's happened to make you say this to me? Do you want me to leave Gail? Is that it?"

I shake my head.

"I'm fifty-three years old. I'm getting to be an old man. What do you want from me? I spend all my money on you. I keep getting you new apartments and jobs. I want the best for you, isn't that obvious? I do everything I can for you. What else do you want from me? That I shouldn't live anymore? Would that make it better?"

I can't think of anything. My mind is as blank as ice. Finally I start to cry and the next thing I know I've fallen like someone falling through ice, only I land in his arms. I keep crying and shaking until I hear him whisper "I'm sorry" in my left ear. I can feel him shaking a little against me like he's crying too. Then I hear three knocks on the door that sound like machine gun fire.

"Don't let her in, Daddy. Please don't let her in," I say over and over. "Don't let her in."

He tells Gail to wait a minute. He tells her he is busy while he continues to hold me. He, my father.

Then the knocking stops.

From the Diary of Gene Mays

Diane's move was a gesture of compromise on both our parts. Since her inheritance and my divorce had both been settled, she saw no reason why we couldn't live together, but I resisted the idea. Instead, she moved into my building and set herself up in an attractive one-room apartment twenty-seven floors beneath me.

Actually, I could afford to live in my building only because of the money I had inherited from my own father three years before. I'm afraid Diane and I were one of those couples who were never successful in the business world and who were paying their way through a fairly comfortable life with gifts from dead fathers.

Diane did have a talent for making friends with people on the fringes of artistic culture in the city, people she invariably invested with far more importance than they deserved. This probably accounted for why they liked her so much and kept inviting her to their parties and gatherings. None of these people were artists, mind you, but they were professors of art or assistant curators, or semi-retired lawyers or music critics for little magazines. That kind of thing. A few weeks after her move we were on our way to a birthday party for a Professor Liza Cedarman, one of the central figures in Diane's circle. I bought the professor a bottle of champagne and pretended to enjoy myself, but a few minutes after arriving a dwarfish anthropology scholar started joking about my living arrangement with Diane. "They're vertically cohabitating," he announced through his laughter, and before I knew it, an entire circle of nitwits was toasting us with my champagne.

Even Diane blushed, although on one level I think the tribute pleased her. I pretended to laugh too, but I used the commotion to slip into the parlor where Professor Cedarman was holding court. Immediately, I was struck by the painting on the wall over her futon. It was an oil painting of a giant orange and pink fish swimming by itself. Both fish and sea were painted semi-abstractly so that it was hard to tell where the fish ended and the ocean began. If you looked at the colors closely you could easily experience a slight hallucination. I found the painting somewhat amateurish yet somewhat appealing.

"I love the painting," I said, eager to say something both flattering and semi-genuine to my hostess.

"It's by my daughter."

"Is she here in Philadelphia?"

"No, right now she's living in some kind of art community in the Berkshires. But she's done so many of these things that she gives me some whenever she visits. She just doesn't have enough space for them all, I guess."

I sensed from her tone that Liza Cedarman didn't think that much of the painting, yet I pressed on with my compliments.

"It's an amazing painting. What a conception of a fish."

"Some people see a series of curvaceous women where the fish scales are. Do you?" asked a dour-faced doctor (an organist by avocation) who sat next to Liza.

"He's much too preoccupied with me to see other women anywhere," said Diane, suddenly appearing in the room. She was accompanied by the dwarfologist, who added, "Especially since he's begun vertically cohabitating."

There was another round of laughter. I praised the painting again and Liza Cedarman said, "Why don't you take it? I have so many of them I barely have enough space to store them myself. Besides, I'd love for you to have it. My daughter will be tickled."

Of course I protested. It was too generous; it was preposterous (I figured the painting's market value might be as high as two or three hundred dollars). But she was adamant. I'm not exactly sure of her motives even now, but everyone in the room was also awed by her generosity, and thin-lipped Liza Cedarman smiled broadly, drinking it in.

That night Diane helped me staple the painting to the wall above my bed. There had been nothing there but a fraying poster of New York, a keepsake from a weekend with Diane. (She loved to travel for fun, whereas it always made me more nervous than happy and later vaguely disappointed as well.) Diane expressed some regret that I was taking down the poster, but on balance she was in too good a mood to complain much. She'd had a wonderful time at the party and complimented me on how polite and unusually animated I'd been. The next morning when she left to go shopping and do some errands (she was a genius at creating errands) she was still in a good mood.

There was really nothing of interest on my other walls, so I was able to look at the painting for perhaps a half-hour. I saw many colors in it that I hadn't noticed before; for example, the bright purples and greens and a whole rainbow of blues. I saw how the fish and water both shimmered and saw the women in the scales and many other things. When the colors began to vibrate strongly, I finally turned away.

There is definitely something magical about this painting, I thought. Then I looked around my apartment and saw the chaos of my desk, my television set resting on its stand as in a coffin, and then the white abomination of my refrigerator, like some hideous robotic snowman. I remember thinking, "There is nothing here that I value except the painting." Was that because there was nothing in my life that I valued either? I thought of my short-lived businesses, all mail-order schemes, never one with even a single full-time employee other than myself. The problem was I could never stand working for other people, but I lacked the drive to succeed on my own. My heart never went into any of these ventures, and with my parents distant but financially generous and always there to bail me out, I'd stop caring each time, so of course the businesses would collapse or wither away.

Well, what of my so-called love life? I was thirty-three. Who had I loved, and who had loved me? My ex-wife was the proverbial big mistake and far more costly than my businesses, as it turned out. My memories of her now chiefly centered around law offices. But what about Diane? We'd met at an art gallery opening (I confess to occasionally enjoying such things) and for no special reason she had set her sights on me. It seems to me I was very passive about it, and a little puzzled as well. Diane was attractive in an angular way. I was not physically attractive in any way, I don't think. Later I thought it was the money she thought I had. Still later I realized that she feasted off my passivity, which made me her perpetual audience and allowed her to be the star of our relationship.

For a while some need of mine must have been filled, as they say, but it had all passed and now was just another mistake to deal with. It was peculiar; I'd once valued Diane, but I wasn't at all curious about why I had and now no longer did. It was as if an infected tooth had been pulled from my head and I'd adjusted immediately to the empty space without any desire to investigate the source of infection.

That doesn't mean that I broke it off with Diane right away. I remained a coward in such matters, still preferring to act poorly and to let my partner get rid of me. It wasn't easy this time either, since Diane was so breezily oblivious to my real nature and was quite used to taking what she wanted from people (including me) while ignoring the rest.

Slowly the painting began to have therapeutic value for me. I often used it as a kind of tranquilizer while Diane was out, or as a diversion while I was forced to have sex with her. Once she caught me in bed looking at it dreamily when, of course, I should have been concentrating on her. A week or so later there was an argument and some insults were exchanged, followed by the returning of keys and other pertinent property.

Hand on slender hip, face white and constricted with witchlike rage, she fired this last shot at me: "In the beginning I thought you had this child-like enthusiasm for things, but now I see you're just a child who can never stick with anything. You go from business to business, from woman to woman, from idea to idea, always thinking there's something better around the corner. I honestly don't know whether to hate you or pity you, but either way, I don't *ever* want to see you again!" Then came the inevitable slamming of the door.

For the next few days I spent much of my time with the painting. It gives me everything, I would say to myself. It relaxes me when I worry, it sweeps me clean of memories (I'd had only one or two of either Diane or my ex-wife), it gives me a constant source of beauty and it uplifts me, filling me with a spiritual sense beyond words that I'd never felt before. I had already committed the painting to memory so that even when I had to leave the apartment to get meals, for instance, I could recall it. I'd also found a way for it to appear fairly regularly in my dreams.

But then this enchanted time (so short, but so exciting and yet strangely peaceful) passed, and my relationship to the painting began to change. It started with the feeling that something was missing in the relationship. By the end of the day I realized it was I myself who was missing: I would always be the painting's adoring audience, while it, of course, could never give me back any attention at all. It's not man who collects paintings, but paintings that passively but inevitably collect and imprison their admirers.

This was a hell of a situation. I lay back in my bed, feeling the kind of dizziness that invariably proceeds my full-blown depressions. "But wait," I thought, suddenly sitting up straight again. "There's a third party involved in all this. There's the painter."

The painting was not a self-actualized entity, after all, but a made thing put together in a matter of days or even hours by a clever, devoted human being. How much more satisfying it might be to meet the creator of the painting, the person who loved it and let it go because she could turn to other paintings, a person perhaps a good deal like myself. In this case such a meeting was entirely possible. It seemed the key not only to rescuing me from my imminent depression, but to much else besides; for Professor Cedarman was a handsome woman, and her daughter might be even more handsome.

A few minutes later I was on the phone to Liza Cedarman. After a minimal amount of small talk I was able to extract her daughter's phone number in Lenox, Massachusetts. At first I thought I'd take some time deciding exactly what I wanted to say to Liza's daughter, whose name was Gretchen. I thought of all kinds of elaborate plans but then decided against them. Since Diane had left, my skills and interest in manipulation had both deteriorated. Instead, I simply picked up the phone one morning and a couple of rings later I was speaking to the painting's creator.

"Gretchen Cedarman?"

"Yes."

"I'm an acquaintance, a friend of your mother, who as you undoubtedly know is an exceedingly generous woman."

There was an uncomfortable silence.

"In fact, I would say she's an astonishingly generous woman since, as you may know, she's given me, as a gift, your extraordinary painting."

Another silence. I was aware that I was being both long winded and convoluted, a nervous habit I'd picked up from my years studying philosophy in graduate school.

"Excuse me. Could you tell me what your name is?"

"Yes, of course. Eugene Mays, but I prefer to be called Gene."

I looked down at my hand, which was trembling. Why did women I cared about sooner or later reduce me to a quivering child?

"Well, thanks for your kind words, Gene."

"I've frankly become extremely interested in your art and I'm wondering if I could see more of your work?"

"My mother's got a lot of them, I think."

"Yes, of course, and I've seen them." This was only half a lie, for I'd noticed a number of other brightly colored ocean paintings fairly similar to mine that night at the party. "It's beautiful work. It has a spiritual quality that deeply affects me. I'm no artist, mind you, but I did study art along with com-

parative religion and philosophy in college. Though in my working life thus far religion has only played a little part, since I'm
a self-employed businessman of a kind. But believe me, I'm
deeply appreciative of your art, more than you can realize. I'm
wondering if I came to Lenox if you could show me more of
your work? I'm interested in writing an article about you, you
see, and my connections in various art circles make me think
there's a good chance it could be published." These last two
statements were a lot closer to being total lies.

"You want to come all the way out here to see my paintings?
Where are you? In Philadelphia?"

"Yes."

"That's a helluva trip to Lenox, Gene, but sure. God, I'm
flattered. Just let me know when you're coming and I'll arrange
my studio. I'll get my fiancé to help me mount the works."

"I'm coming right away, if that's all right with you. I'm coming
as soon as possible."

Yes, I was jealous that there was already someone in her life
to "mount the works," although perhaps she was a little frightened and simply made him up. But I did leave right away as
I'd promised. It was a six-hour drive during which I reviewed
our conversation from every conceivable vantage point and,
incidentally, only saw the painting in my mind's eye a few times.
It was clear to me now that it was the painter, and not her
painting, that I was truly interested in. Though I knew even
before I read the line in school that Hell is other people, I also
knew that Heaven is other people too. As I approached the
green and blue town of Lenox I saw a quick image of Diane's
self-occupied face and thought, "I have definitely had enough
of Hell for a while. In fact, I'm completely ready for Heaven."

Heaven Cedarman, as I began to call her to myself, was living
not in Lenox per se, but in a small community of cottages by
a hill-surrounded lake called Beachwood. Heaven was wearing
blue jeans and a white long-sleeved sweater. (It was the middle
of June, but it got cool in the late country afternoon.) I saw
her first through the screen door of her cottage; her face was
incredibly strong and handsome and framed by hair a shade

darker than mine. When she looked up and saw me I was waving both hands rather comically, I suppose. "Hi! Hi! It's Gene Mays." When Heaven rose to open the door, I noticed an arm suddenly draped around her shoulder like an eel. "Hi, Gene, I'm stunned that you got here so fast. I'm Gretchen, and this is my fiancé, Don Patchen." The eel man extended his hand and I forced myself to shake it. Although she had told me about him on the phone I was still shocked to see him, and disgusted by how incessantly physical he was with her, as if he had to be touching a different part of her every two seconds. For a few minutes there was some uninspired conversation about roads and highways, while I kept my eyes fixed on Gretchen.

The sun is a cruel photographer—how else to explain that what seemed so handsome in her face when I saw it through the screen door now seemed merely striking or faintly bizarre. Her eyes were still impressively large, for example, but so were her other features. The net result was that she looked a bit like one of those oversized neoclassic heads of Picasso's. I also saw that while she was fairly tall she was not actually as tall as I was, nor was her hair any darker than my own.

We walked to her studio, formerly a smallish garage beside her cottage. The eel man kept patting her on the rump, while Gretchen responded each time with some new tribute to him. Really, he was like a puppeteer perversely prompting her to keep spewing forth his name into the atmosphere. I noticed during her entire conversation she didn't mention her mother once.

The paintings were full of the same oranges and pinks, mauves and turquoise blues as mine, and most of them were also of water environments with fish or flowers floating in them. There were some powerful sections, but many more garish or unfocused ones, the total effect being uncomfortably adolescent.

Of course, I tried to hide my disappointment. I heaped praise on those works I half admired. I even pretended to take a few notes for that prospective article I'd mentioned, but all the while I was making plans to escape from them, and when Gretchen asked me in for a drink I already had an excuse ready. I also told her that I'd decided to have my article concentrate exclusively on the painting her mother had given me, though I assured her that seeing these others had helped. Gretchen looked perplexed. Even after my detailed description she wasn't sure which fish painting I had in my apartment; she'd done so many.

"Well, let me know what happens with the article, and call me if you need any, you know, biographical information about me." I nodded and assured her I would. A few minutes later I was shaking her hand and then the eel man's and backing into my car, which, in turn, backed up her dirt driveway and out onto another dirt road.

"Well, that was a grotesque disappointment," I said to myself as I headed off in no particular direction. It was peculiar; whenever I'd felt as hysterical as I was feeling then, my mind invariably raced with thoughts, or at least circled in repetitive patterns, but this time it was completely blank. It was as if I'd become a mere receptacle for pain that was welling up within me, without a single idea or thought to use in my own defense. To make matters worse, I was completely lost in a labyrinth of dirt roads, befuddled and exasperated.

How swift was Heaven's fall, how eternal are the roads of Hell, I thought with all the romantic bitterness of which I was capable, which was quite a lot. Then I turned again, and a miraculous thing happened. I, Gene, lost in a maze, at last saw a clearing, a little gray beach that led to a smallish lake. Immediately my throbbing headache disappeared, and I was filled with a kind of bliss I hadn't felt since I was a child. I knew in an instant I had to get out of the car. The only way I can describe what I felt next is that I had somehow stepped into paradise. Tears came to my eyes, then an enveloping smile. How wonderful the sand was! It was the very pavement of paradise. I kept picking it up and tossing it in the air like confetti as I ran down to the water's edge. The blue-gray lake rippled slightly in the cool wind. I felt like it was allowing me to think again, but on a much higher level than I had ever thought before. I've lost everything now, I thought: my parents, my wife, Diane. I've also lost the painting, in a way, and now the painter. I've lost exactly what I thought would save me—yet I feel unaccountably happy. How can this be? But, of course, I was looking at the answer. I quickly threw off my shoes and waded out to the white wooden dock with all my clothes on. Magically, the water stopped at my neck. I suppose I was shivering, but I hardly cared. After all, I was solving a mystery that had lasted as long as my life. As I climbed up the ladder to the dock a blue gill nipped my toes, and then it seemed I'd finished solving the mystery as I finally sat gazing out at the holy lake.

No wonder Plato had such a low opinion of artists who merely create images of things. No wonder I couldn't find what I needed in either the painting or its painter—it's the thing itself I needed. Water, the very fluid of God, where life emerged and foolishly fled, relegating it, in all too many cases like my own, to a mere vacation site.

I'm getting too frantic. I'm thinking too fast, I thought, so I dipped my feet into the water again. Joy shot through me completely and instantly, and I calmed down and was able to make decisions. I would sell my hideous apartment and move near the ocean; for the lake was in a way an image of the ocean and, transcendent as the lake was, it was the ocean I really yearned for. Naturally, I would eventually need to find work— my savings could last perhaps two more years. So what were the possibilities? Could I be a lifeguard, for instance? I was too scrawny (and probably old) and swam too poorly, and even if I built myself up enough to qualify, there might be too many distractions at the beach. A lighthouse keeper would be much more appropriate, though I understood that job was almost a thing of the past; it was all done by machines now. Could I perhaps pilot a cruise boat or something of the sort? Certainly I could learn, though I'm sure there were little mafias controlling that business too, and it might be very difficult to break in.

The future was full of problems but I felt they would eventually take care of themselves. A revelation is worth a million problems, after all, and I'd already learned the essential thing and made the most important decision.

I closed my eyes and lay down on the dock over the lake like a man over a lover he never wants to leave. For a while the water seemed to speak directly to me, saying, "This is the source of life, this is where God is," over and over as it kept rolling in. But all too quickly that blissful time passed. While I was still calm I began to think, "If only this were the ocean, where one can hear not just the half-audible (half-imagined) whispers but the umistakable roar of God. If only I were there, I would be sure of what I was hearing. Then I'd really be someplace." So, yes, I was still haunted by a regret. After an hour of debating about it I ultimately climbed down the ladder and waded back to shore, ready to start my life's new plan in earnest.

Lenox is not near any ocean. Fortunately, it did have plenty of stores that sold towels and bathing suits, both of which I purchased, along with a sweatshirt. I had to pay for them with my water-logged money, but I managed to endure a few smart comments about my drenched condition from both the cashier and a fellow shopper before heading straight for the car, where I was finally able to change into my new (dry) outfit. I could have reached Cape Cod in an hour and a half of inspired driving. Instead, knowing only what I knew at the time, I decided to head for the Jersey shore. I didn't think about anything except the ocean once my ride began. Like everyone else, I'd loved it as a kid but had moved away and hadn't even been to a beach in a couple of years. I'd been to the Jersey shore, though, and I remembered how big the waves were there; you could body surf almost like you could in California. The procession of rolling, crashing waves that I saw in my mind's eye kept me company during my long trip, until these remembered waves began to have a hypnotic effect and I pulled over to an anonymous-looking motel. I wanted to stay just a few hours so I could catch the sun rising over the ocean, but apparently I was more tired than I realized. When I got up the next day it was already mid-morning.

Small matter. So I wouldn't see the sun rise on the first day of my new life. Big deal. I mocked myself for my absurd perfectionism and continued driving, charged with energy and focused singlemindedly on any shortcuts to the sea.

I arrived at Ventnor Beach (adjacent to Atlantic City and much more charming) at 12:45. But why should I think of the fine distinction between the two beaches? Why congratulate myself on driving the extra two miles to Ventnor when the same God-stunned ocean roared and laughed in front of both? I tried to keep my level of inspiration up by focusing on the endless churning bar of blue before me as I ran down the sand to embrace it. I couldn't run in anything like a straight line, for there were lots of people on the beach playing Frisbee or lying on their stomachs sunning themselves, or striking poses in their suits as they preened and flirted and tried to pick each other up. I wanted to yell at them with all the strength of my lungs to go in the water with me, but first I had to save myself.

For twenty minutes it was ecstasy. I swam, I went underwater, I played with the waves like a porpoise. I rubbed water into my hair and skin, I floated. Then I began to get a little tired; also I started to shiver. Maybe there were so few people swimming because the water was so cold. Some clouds came out, covering the sun, and it grew even colder. I started to swim to shore, but halfway there I felt tired and half floated the rest of the way. Somehow the undertow made me drift toward a scrawny kid with yellow hair who was busily and unapologetically peeing into the sea. I choked with rage when I saw this and had to fight off the desire to slap his face and/or strangle him. Quickly I turned away and swam to shore, still shaking with anger and fear.

I had come perilously close to hitting a child while bathing in God's water. What was the matter with me? What had happened to my vision? I paced along the beach, trying to find an isolated spot to think it all out, but it was impossible. People had multiplied, their transistor radios blaring, their ice cream cones dripping, their Frisbees hitting each other, their garbage accumulating. One boy alone was being quiet; he was doing a crayon drawing of the ocean. This ordinary-looking and ordinarily skilled adolescent stopped me in my tracks. The chaos in my head began to unravel. I have come full circle, I thought, as I watched him color in the waves.

People are treating the beach and ocean this way because they know God isn't there any longer. They know on some level what Plato (now that I thought more carefully about him) knew: the entire physical universe is an image, a painting, if you will, of the archetypes. That's why there's no lasting satisfaction or relief in the physical world. I felt imprisoned, infinitely helpless, the victim of a cosmic mirage. Stunned, I sat down on the sand near the boy artist and tried to go through the steps again in my mind.

The Earth is God's painting, but God is not directly in the painting anymore and, possibly like Gretchen, who couldn't exactly recall which fish painting I owned, God no longer remembers this particular painting we call the Earth. I thought of empty space. Maybe that was God's home? No, it too was a painting; empty space had its archetype as well. These people playing or showing off on the beach instinctively realized this. They were not to be despised; they were simply passing time. I was the fool, and in Ventnor I had come to the end of my line. I buried my head, I shivered. I felt constricted with pain and closed my eyes and cried a fool's tears. Only then did I start to feel better.

To think, Democritus tore out his eyes. Yes, from Homer to Milton to Borges we have always regarded blind men as sages. Why? Because they were no longer hypnotized by the painting, they alone could reach the archetype. However, I could not rush into this. If I had learned anything in these strange days, it was that I had quite an amazing capacity to be wrong. No, I needn't blind myself, but I could keep my eyes closed much more often— through sleep, and through meditation. I could keep my ears closed, too, for sounds were also hypnotic and addictive. I made a mental note to check out the sensory deprivation research in Center City.

Yet, I might not even need to do that, I thought, as I slowly headed back to my car. What I needed to do was drive home, disconnect my phones, pull the drapes, apply a sleeping mask and ear plugs to my head, and then finally begin to try to pierce through the painting. The blind knew, or at least the enlightened blind knew (for of course there were blind people who were stupid too) that if God lives anywhere, He lives behind the walls and mirrors of phenomena.

I became tremendously excited about the possibilities of all this and soon was running toward my car, my new purpose clearly before me. Just before I left I did look back once more. I saw a giant wave breaking from which a fish seemed to jump, although it might actually have been a little child or his raft. The next thing I knew I was driving again, dreaming of the time when I could finally close my long-suffering, long-deceived eyes.

ILLINOIS SHORT FICTION